COMMITMENT TO SUSTAINABILITY

Ooligan Press is committed to becoming an academic leader in sustainable publishing practices. Using both the classroom and the business, we will investigate, promote, and utilize sustainable products, technologies, and practices as they relate to the production and distribution of our books. We hope to lead and encourage the publishing community by our example. Making sustainable choices is not only vital to the future of our industry—it's vital to the future of our world.

OPENBOOK SERIES

One component of our sustainability campaign is the OpenBook Series. Siblings and Other Disappointments is the _____ book in the series, so named to highlight our commitment to transparency on our road toward sustainable publishing. We believe that disclosing the impacts of the choices we make will not only help us avoid unintentional greenwashing, but also serve to educate those who are unfamiliar with the choices available to printers and publishers. Efforts to produce this series as sustainably as possible focus on paper and ink sources, design strategies, efficient and safe manufacturing methods, innovative printing technologies, supporting local and regional companies, and corporate responsibility of our contractors. All titles in the OpenBook Series will have the OpenBook logo on the front cover and a corresponding OpenBook Environmental Audit inside, which includes a calculated paper impact from the Environmental Paper Network.

SIBLINGS AND OTHER DISAPPOINTMENTS AUDIT

For Ooligan Press, our commitment to sustainability in publishing considers not only environmental outcomes, but economic and social impacts as well. Through the short-run printing process for *Siblings and Other Disappointments*, the decision to opt for a shorter print run than usual allows for less paper and carbon use and greater economic sustainability. By preserving sustainable printing practices in a concentrated amount, we increase accountability with less extraneous books printed.

Additionally, this printing contributes to the region's cultural sustainability by highlighting a feminist voice and championing the narratives of women writers. We strive to continue this history of cultural impact by focusing on economic savings and sustainable publishing practices that maintain high standards for quality. Ooligan Press is proud to introduce its newest addition to the OpenBook Series, an initiative that continues to think beyond the page and seek innovation in environmental, economic, and social contributions to conscious practices for the present and future of publishing.

PRAISE FOR SIBLINGS AND OTHER DISAPPOINTMENTS:

"Heacock's stories feel like tiny homecomings, like peering in the windows of the real Northwest and glimpsing its shabby, secret heart. These characters' poignancy is in the smallness of their desires: to sit down again at the same counter; to be seen; to touch hands across the darkness, even as time makes them—and all of us—obsolete." —Megan Kruse, *Call Me Home*

"Kait Heacock's stories map a meticulous landscape of loneliness. Whether she's exploring the lives of two people who live in the same house but communicate only through scribbled confessions, of a father whose gambling addiction blinds him to the needs of his daughter, or of a mother praying for the end of the world, she's attuned to both the intricacies of isolation and the elusive connections—often internal ones—that stave off despair. *Siblings and Other Disappointments* is a stark, honest, and moving collection." —Scott Nadelson, *Aftermath* and *Between You and Me*

"Twelve stories of wounds and disappointments—Kait Heacock's debut story collection, *Siblings and Other Disappointments*, winds through fractures and futile hopes, broken promises and loneliness, exploring all the ways family—however it's defined—can simultaneously be comforting and terrible. Each story in the collection is painful in its own way, and yet there's hope to be found, too, and certainly beauty. As a whole, *Siblings and Other Disappointments* skillfully explores the space between what we want our families to be and what our families actually are." —Nicole Wolverton, *The Trajectory of Dreams*

"Kait Heacock's Pacific Northwest is full of fractured families trying to repair themselves, wayward children making incomplete sense of their parents' foibles and grief, a mother waiting patiently for the Rapture, and a father bonding with his daughter over a Mac Attack Stack Challenge. These are closely observed, unsentimental stories about parents, children, husbands, and wives finding their uncertain way after wreckage has laid them low. Yet the heartache at the center of these stories is leavened by Heacock's clear-eyed compassion and humor. This finely crafted debut collection heralds an important new voice in the literary West." —K. L. Cook, *The Girl from Charnelle* and *Last Call*

"The close-up character studies in Kait Heacock's stories are full of real-life pain, sadness, and desire. Although there are a lot of heartbreaking goodbyes throughout *Siblings and Other Disappointments*, the encouraging thing is that this book is one hearty hello to an impressive new storyteller." —Kevin Sampsell, *This Is Between Us* and *A Common Pornography*

SIBLINGS
AND OTHER DISAPPOINTMENTS

SIBLINGS
AND OTHER DISAPPOINTMENTS

STORIES
KAIT HEACOCK

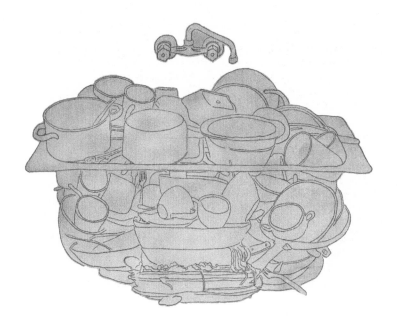

Ooligan
PRESS

Portland, Oregon

Siblings and Other Disappointments
© 2016 Kait Heacock

ISBN13: 978-1-932010-85-5

Ooligan Press
Portland State University
Post Office Box 751, Portland, Oregon 97207
503.725.9748
ooligan@ooliganpress.pdx.edu
www.ooliganpress.pdx.edu

Library of Congress Cataloging-in-Publication Data
Names: Heacock, Kait, author.
Title: Siblings and other disappointments / Kait Heacock.
Description: Portland, Oregon : Ooligan Press, 2016.
Identifiers: LCCN 2016012497 (print) | LCCN 2016023763 (ebook) | ISBN 9781932010855 (trade paper : alk. paper) | ISBN 9781932010862 (ebook)
Subjects: LCSH: Families--Fiction. | Disappointment--Fiction. | Psychological fiction. | Domestic fiction.
Classification: LCC PS3608.E225 A6 2016 (print) | LCC PS3608.E225 (ebook) | DDC 813/.6--dc23
LC record available at https://lccn.loc.gov/2016012497

Cover design by Ryan Brewer
with production assistance by Leigh Thomas and Cade Hoover
Interior design by Leigh Thomas

References to website URLs were accurate at the time of writing. Neither the author nor Ooligan Press is responsible for URLs that have changed or expired since the manuscript was prepared.

Printed in the United States of America

For Justy

CONTENTS

UPSTAIRS

Peter was an agoraphobic. He couldn't explain what that was a year ago, but he could describe now what it was like to stand by the front door and feel the heat radiate off the knob, so sure it could burn you if you touched it. He couldn't explain his newly diagnosed panic attacks, but he knew that going outside triggered them, so he stopped. He never would have guessed when he rented this one-bedroom basement apartment that it could become his waking coffin, that he would let her death bury him alive. It was the first place he found on Craigslist; the woman who owned the house was the first landlord to return his call, and he took it without inspecting the toilet or looking closer at the cracks in the ceiling.

Sylvia didn't know she had rented the apartment in her basement to an agoraphobic. She thought they kept different hours.

As a nurse who worked the graveyard shift three nights a week, she had grown used to keeping hours with truck drivers, ghosts, and the women working on Highway 99. She had become a ghost herself at some point. She lost track of when.

Sylvia didn't sleep most nights. Working as a nurse gave her an excuse some nights; the others, she hadn't noticed. She discovered she was an insomniac as she fried a pan of corn tortilla strips for migas and saw that the clock on the microwave said four a.m.

Peter had walked into the apartment two weeks after the mugging. It wasn't until he had finished unpacking and looked out the window at the wet snow and gray slush of January that he realized he never wanted to leave again. The therapist who visited him on Wednesdays stamped him with post-traumatic stress disorder. Peter's father paid a lot of money for the therapist to make house calls. Peter's father expected a quick turnaround.

"Be a man, son," he said after three months. "When your mother died..."

"You were already married to your new wife," Peter reminded him.

After six months in the apartment, a check came in the mail every month from his father, and his phone calls came less than that.

Sylvia looked for remedies to sleeplessness in warm milk, baths, and advice posted on online forums. She had Ambien pushed on her but didn't want to *need* a medicine. The night after an orderly gave her a joint to relax her, she spent four hours sitting on the kitchen counter and ate an entire box of Cheerios.

The hours she didn't spend sleeping afforded her extra time for thinking. She remembered her mamá always finding time to cook the family breakfast even though she left for her shift at the hospital in Sunnyside before Sylvia and her brothers boarded the bus for school. She thought of the thousand small ways mothers make sacrifices—so many before their children have the words to ask for them. She thought about her divorce twenty years ago (for making such a mortal sin, her mamá didn't speak to her for a year after), whether she regretted never having children, and how lonely the end of your life can become when there is nobody around at night.

The technicalities of agoraphobia were easy for Peter to work out. He ordered groceries online and, when they arrived, called his friends over to bring them inside. His stepsister dropped in once or twice a month with bulk toilet paper and weed. He insulated the windows to prevent any outside air from seeping through like poisonous gas. The dog door put in by the previous renters was carefully sealed with duct tape. The outside world came in quick gusts when visitors opened the front door, but even then, Peter usually stood in his bedroom to keep that wind from touching his skin.

Realizing she had no way of overcoming her insomnia, Sylvia took up hobbies. She painted watercolors, made scrapbooks, knit hats and scarves for her sobrinos, tried playing poker online, and wrote letters to the editors of the *Seattle Times*. No hobby had managed to hold her attention for more than a few weeks. She felt satisfied that she could accomplish so much in such a short amount of time and thought of all the other activities she had spent her life hoping to learn, like French cooking. But inevitably, somewhere around three a.m., she found herself pacing her living room.

Peter had only met his landlord twice, once to look at the place and the second time to exchange payment for the key. His rent checks went out the door with his visitors, and he had no need to call her down into his apartment. After a while her face had faded from his memory until she became a series of noises.

At first, he hadn't noticed how much she'd grown to be a part of his life. Her noises had become ingrained in his routine: On Mondays, Wednesdays, and Fridays (the nights she worked the graveyard shift), he awoke when she came home, flipped over onto his stomach as she set her keys onto the kitchen counter and turned on the faucet, and fell back asleep knowing that the sun wouldn't rise for a few more hours. On the nights she wasn't working, he could hear her favorite television shows, the smoke detector beeping when she cooked, and occasionally her voice on the telephone. The sound of her voice comforted him, like his favorite teacher or aunt.

The nights became longer as he adapted to her schedule. During the day, when she worked, he could bask in the silence from above and feel guiltless about spending time alone, something he had suppressed most of his life. But at night, her footsteps became the ticking of the clock, the rhythm of a heartbeat, unrelenting—night after night. He caught her sleeplessness like a cold. He thought about pounding on his ceiling with a broom. It reminded him of his dorm-room days, and he didn't want to resort to that. He couldn't ask the woman to stop walking in her own apartment. But why was she pacing? Why didn't she sleep?

The pacing started out as a tactic to tire her, but after a month it developed into something else. It was a mild workout (she thought her clothes felt looser than usual), it was a stress reliever, and it was *something* to pass the time. One night she paced her living room for three hours. Then she started to count her steps, and with the repetition of the numbers in her head and the sound of her feet hitting the hardwood floor, she managed to quiet her restless mind. She couldn't sleep, but for the first time, she began to enjoy the peacefulness of night.

Sometimes it seemed like the footsteps were getting louder. Was she jumping rope? Was she tap dancing? Didn't she know he could hear the floorboards lurching with every step?

One night, he finished the last of his beer and opened the bottle of whiskey he kept on reserve. He sat on the couch in his boxers, clinked the ice in his glass, and listened. After he was fairly drunk, he felt convinced that this woman was trying to tell him something. This woman upstairs somehow held the secret of what he was supposed to do with his life now, but he couldn't get to her. So he listened. He thought perhaps her footsteps were sending a message, like Morse code. He looked it up online and tried to follow the dots and dashes of her walking with the chart he pulled up on his screen. He abandoned this plan when he realized he couldn't hear dashes, all dots.

When his therapist came that week and he told her about the woman upstairs, she nodded vigorously, almost enthusiastically, as if his new obsession were a healthy step forward.

"Maybe you could try talking to her, call her on the phone, perhaps," she suggested.

"And tell her what? That I haven't left the house in over nine months, that I am scared to go outside again because every time I even think of it, I picture my dead girlfriend's face? Do you think she'll let me sign the lease for another year if I tell her that?"

Sylvia counted one thousand steps one night and felt like she had accomplished something. Next time she'd try for fifteen hundred.

It happened during the day, when the apartment was quiet and he felt especially lonely. Instead of passively listening—to her footsteps, to her muffled phone calls, or to her teakettle whistling—Peter finally realized he wanted to talk back. After months of his family, his friends, and his therapist prodding for answers to everything from how he felt to what he planned to do next, it dawned on him that the only person he cared to talk to knew him only through a check in her mailbox. There was no guarantee she could hear him. People above rarely listen to those below, and it was not like she would ever put her ear to the ground. The best he could do was write to her.

He had been raised Catholic; a confession felt the most appropriate. He wasn't ready to talk about it, the thing everyone wanted to hear. He wanted to start small, someplace far back, a secret he had never told anyone before.

When Peter's friend stopped by with a bag of groceries, Peter handed him an envelope with his rent check and a square one the size of a thank-you card, blank save for his landlord's name written in his best cursive.

"What's the blank one for?" his friend asked.

"It's a note to her. She's been keeping me up at night. It's just a neighborly comment on noise level," he lied. "Put it in her mailbox behind the check."

He felt right just knowing that his secret had entered the world. He pictured it growing wings. He pictured his landlord holding it and plucking its feathers.

Sylvia came home from work feeling exhausted. It was flu season, and she had spent most of the day giving shots to people who sneezed on her. The stack of mail she threw on the table looked average. She saw her cable bill and a reminder from her dentist of her approaching six-month checkup. She opened the envelope from her tenant and put the folded rent check into her wallet. Then she saw the small white envelope with only her first name on it.

When she opened the envelope and looked at the scribbled note, she assumed it to be some kind of dirty joke. *When I was twelve, I masturbated thinking about my stepsister.* She looked around her to make sure nobody was peeking into her window, laughing. She threw the paper into the recycling bin, stopped for a moment, pulled it back out, and ripped it in half before throwing it in the trash.

Whether his landlord knew the notes came from him or not wasn't the point. The point was getting it all out. *I cheated on the SATs* appeared two weeks after the first note. *I never once attended my microeconomics class sophomore year* came at the end of the month. *I was the one who puked all over my friend's car* was dropped off after only a week. He had his friends put them in the mailbox faster, without even the pretense of accompanying the rent check. *I cheated on my junior-year girlfriend when I studied abroad* was followed a few days later by *I've never forgiven my father for leaving my mother.*

Sylvia had found her distraction, something on which to focus her directionless time and energy. The letters appeared in her mail like tiny Christmas gifts. Each one's arrival was a sign that she was not as alone as she feared; at the very least, someone else was as alone as she felt. She stored them safely next to the saint candles she hadn't lit since her mother passed: Santa Teresa, Santa Martha, and her favorite, Santa Barbara. She was building an altar out of someone else's sins.

When they started coming more frequently, she began to anticipate them daily, like when she used to anticipate sleep. She thought she knew where they were coming from, considered setting up surveillance on her front porch, but finally gave up and let them be tokens from a generous ghost.

I am afraid to leave my apartment. I haven't left since I moved in. I am trapped.

Peter didn't want to be coy anymore. This time he slipped the note inside the envelope with his rent check. He stopped licking the adhesive on the envelope halfway through and pulled the note out. He scribbled *help me* along the bottom of it.

Sylvia's lack of sleep finally caught up with her at work. She fell asleep beside her patient's bed and missed administering medicine. It wasn't fatal, but it was enough to earn her a month's suspension for negligence as well as the suggestion of early retirement.

"Now you'll have all the free time you could want to pick up a new hobby or catch up on your reading. You'll have nothing but time," she was told.

She accepted this assumption of her senility because she didn't want her coworkers to know the truth—that she had been living many years in a waking dream state. She tried to remember if there were other times she had nodded off at work and realized that, as lucid as she thought she was during the day, she was only really awake at night. She had been sleepwalking through the rest of her life.

Sylvia needed a letter that evening. She opened her mailbox eagerly and sifted through credit card offers and grocery store coupons until she found it. This envelope felt heavier. It puffed like a little pillow. She ran inside, threw the rest of her mail on the counter, and sat down to open it. She pulled at one corner and, when it loosened, slid the tip of her finger from one side to the other. She unfolded the letter and had to read the first sentence a few times to make sure she had read it right. *It's my fault my girlfriend died.*

Peter and his girlfriend had been out at a bar on Capitol Hill that night. They drank too much in celebration of his acceptance into the University of Washington's Graduate School of Architecture. Neither could drive. They took a taxi and made a pact that they would wake up early enough the next morning to retrieve his car before it was ticketed.

They lived in an apartment close to Aurora. One of these days, Peter thought, when they made more money and after she finished law school and he had his architect's license, they would move somewhere better, away from the noise and the half-lit neon signs. At first when they saw the man hovering on the sidewalk they thought he was homeless. He stood between them and their front door. Peter turned and watched the taxi pull away.

When he turned back, he saw the man holding a gun. Peter's girlfriend tensed up beside him. The man breathed booze in their faces and yelled at them to hand over their wallets. They did, but he still didn't leave. He moved closer, coughed in Peter's face. An ambulance passed in the distance; its sirens distracted the man.

Peter shoved his girlfriend forward, toward the apartment building. "Just run." He didn't know why he had said it. He didn't know then and he hadn't figured it out yet.

The man turned and shot her. When she dropped to her knees, the man ran. He had shot her in the back so that the last thing she saw before she died was her home.

Sylvia didn't receive any more letters after that. She knew the ghost downstairs was done talking. Now it was time for him to leave. It was in the middle of the night when it occurred to her how best to exorcise him. She walked through her living room, drinking a glass of red wine and lighting every saint candle. She stopped to recite the prayer to Santa Barbara: "A ti vengo, en fé, confiado en tu intercesion." Then she sat down and lit a cigarette. She hadn't smoked in years, probably not since she was going through her divorce. The cigarette tasted like a stale memory.

A yawn slipped out of her mouth, and she giggled at the surprise of it. Her mouth stretched wide to let out another. She thought of the old saying "I'll sleep when I'm dead" and felt relieved. She dropped the cigarette onto the rug and closed her eyes.

The smell of smoke did not wake Peter. It was the smoke detector's incessant whine that pulled him from bed. He reached over and swatted at his alarm. When he knocked it to the ground and the noise still didn't stop, he sat up in bed. Then he smelled the smoke. He threw on his bathrobe and ran for the kitchen. Peter checked the microwave, checked the stove, and realized the smoke came from upstairs. He walked through his kitchen to the front door. He had not passed through it since he moved in, and he wasn't sure he wanted to now. The smoke filled the room, filled his lungs, and he coughed so hard it felt like his chest was ripping apart. He thought he could hear sirens, but he wasn't sure they would make it to him in time.

Peter bent down on his knees and peeled the duct tape off the dog door. He threw the tape in little balls onto the kitchen floor. He put one hand on the ground and the other on the little door. He pushed it open and felt the cool air. The smoke detector in the kitchen buzzed in his ear. He reached for the knob, but pulled back. He pushed the dog door open again and moved his face toward the opening. He breathed deeply the outside, breathed until his lungs were full.

SIRENS

The waves keep me up. It's not fear of a storm or the fear of capsizing or the fear when I think of the boat drifting out to sea. It's not the seasickness, which I've gotten under control by now. It's not even Marco's snoring, which starts out softer, more erratic, like a sputtering engine that won't start, then gets going full throttle—the one unattractive feature about this Adonis-like man. No, it's not Marco's snoring keeping me awake.

It's the waves that I listen to now, the way they roar when they hit the side of Captain's boat like they're trying to push us out of their way. It's the repetition of a sleep-sound machine, only more threatening because the waves can't be turned off. It's the build, the release. The build, the release. I'm jealous of the waves and their purpose. I envy their release.

The problem is, I'm all build since we pushed out of Valdez. It's just Captain, Marco, and me. There is no privacy on a boat with two other people when you all share one room. I'm so blue my balls look like the ocean. Captain and Marco use the Jerk-Off Parlor, as Captain has adeptly nicknamed it. There's only the one bathroom on the boat, so whenever you use it, the other two men will know if you're showering, shitting, or spanking the monkey. Captain decked out the bathroom with torn out pages from *Playboy* and *Penthouse*—a barrage of tits and ass that he rotates out when he returns from his fishing trips and stocks up on supplies in Anchorage. The only one that never moves is the spread of Anna Nicole Smith from *Playboy* in the nineties.

"Don't touch Anna. That's the one rule of the Jerk-Off Parlor. She's my old standby when nothing else will do the trick," Captain explained when I boarded his fishing boat at the start of June, a week after graduation. "I don't normally take on kids your age. At eighteen, you want to tear it up in Anchorage, chase pussy, get your hands on booze. My boat requires hard work. I make my living off this salmon. Do you hear that, Kevin? This is my livelihood. Don't screw this up," Captain explained, then put his hand on my shoulder and squeezed it. "And don't fuck with my Anna. She's the only thing that keeps me sane out here, the only woman who can. She's outlasted my two marriages."

My dad knows Captain from the navy. My dad has dozens of old friends from his navy days, but they're scattered around the world or else dead. Once a year he and my mom would drive to Reno to visit a couple of his closest buddies and their wives or girlfriends. It's like a brotherhood, a fraternity I'll never belong to—not like I'd want to pledge in the first place.

Captain's been up here in Alaska commercially fishing for as long as my dad's been in Washington working in security. Dad started out as a security guard and worked his way up to middle management. Now he oversees over one hundred security guards, many of them vets themselves, some from the Gulf War like Dad and some from as far back as Vietnam, while others are newly booted from Iraq or Afghanistan and looking for a place to land. My dad says security is a great place for vets to go when they return from deployment. He's told me more than once how he made a comfortable life for himself, my mom, and me.

"And all that for not having more than a high school diploma," he loves to add.

I hate Dad most of the time. Admiral Fucking Asshole, always on my case about my art. I picked up drawing as a kid, doodling in the margins of my notebook paper during class, earning my best grades in art. My high school art teacher, Mr. Johnson, was the one who encouraged me to really pursue it. He's the one who turned me onto charcoals.

"You're going to an art institute? They don't have the decency to call it a university? My parents leave behind their families and country so their grandson can *study* art?" Dad asked when I came home with an acceptance letter from the Art Institute of Seattle, three hundred miles away from him.

"Yes, art."

"You know this won't cover everything," he said and waved my scholarship letter around like evidence. Mom stood silently behind him while he lectured me. Mom's tactic for keeping the peace was to stay so quiet you'd think she was willing herself to disappear.

"I'll make up the rest in student loans."

"You can't just heap debt on yourself. You should do the responsible thing and join the military."

Join like he did out of high school—a zealous first generation American attempting to show patriotism for his country. Even if I wanted to, which I don't, I couldn't on the condition that my heart has a hole in it. Not a big one, but enough of a defect that it makes me "unfit for service." My dad thinks I'm defective in a lot of ways.

"Welcome to Anchorage, Kevin. Now, let's get the fuck out of here before my ex-wives find out I'm here." That's how Captain introduced himself to me when he picked me up from the airport. He had a white beard and wore a blue knit cap pulled down tight over his head. "My exes can smell me when I'm in town. Maybe it's the fish they smell on me, but I think they can smell my money underneath that." Captain did most of the talking as we drove to Valdez. "This is the largest port in Alaska, the most important. We'll be fishing in the Prince William Sound. See those mountains in the distance? Those are the Chugach Mountains. They're about two hundred fifty miles long. Because of their location on the Gulf of Alaska, they receive the most snowfall in the world. You hear that, Kevin? The whole fucking world." As he rambled on, in a lazy drawl that sounded like he must have originated in the South, I tuned him out and followed his pointing finger toward the mountain, jagged razors cutting the horizon.

My dad said Alaska would make me feel like a man. My dad was convinced I needed to feel like a man.

Captain explained our geography—Prince William Sound, where we'd be salmon fishing, and Valdez, his home, with a population of less than four thousand people. While he talked, I thought of the brief and horrific research I had done two weeks earlier when I learned I was being shipped off to Alaska to spend the summer fishing before leaving for school in August. My research was grim: of the nearly one thousand work-related deaths in Alaska between 1990 and 2008 (eighteen years, the number of years I'd been alive), one-third were fishermen.

"Most of the surrounding land is part of the Chugach National Forest, which is the second-largest national forest in the US,"

Captain explained. He had a picture of Poseidon, god of the sea, on his bicep that I watched flex and relax as he steered.

The fourth most common cause of death for fishermen is diving-related.

Captain: "We're in Southcentral Alaska, the most populous region in Alaska. That's only because of Anchorage."

The third most common cause of death for fishermen is on-board injuries.

Captain: "The average temperature in Valdez is about sixty degrees Fahrenheit this time of year. So you won't freeze your balls off, Kevin, but don't expect to be a bathing beauty either. You'll be working all day, and you'll be tired as fuck at night. Most nights, you'll be too tired even to rub one out. You can try, but you'll probably fall asleep with your dick out."

The second most common means of death for fishermen is falling overboard.

Captain: "Don't fall asleep with your dick out, Kevin. You're bunking with Marco, and I'm in the cabin too. We don't want to see your dick."

The number one reason for fatalities on fishing boats is death after a vessel disaster.

I didn't know who Marco was, nor did my dad. For all Dad knew, it would just be Captain and me. But the Captain, even with a Gillnet boat, still needed two people to help him.

"Marco Arellano meet Kevin Yu," he said, stretching out the "yoo" sound and looking pleased with his pronunciation. "Kevin's from Washington. Kennewick, right Kevin? Marco here is from Los Angeles. He's a tough piece of shit," Captain said when we boarded the boat the next day and found Marco sitting and smoking a cigarette. He was shirtless and had sleeve tattoos on both arms. He had an anchor on his left pec.

"Hey, Kevin. Nice to meet you," Marco said and noticed me eyeing his artwork. "I put this here so any girl would know from now on, without a question, what my first love is. I got it after my first summer here. Stick around long enough and you'll fall in love too."

Some of the ink on his arms was pretty good. I thought the anchor was a cliché. Maybe I hated sea tattoos because of my dad. He had an anchor on his right bicep.

"Hey, man. Nice to meet you too," I said, standing up straight and slapping his hand in greeting.

"Marco, how many years you been fishing with me?" Captain asked him.

Marco, with a far-off look like he was thinking back, said, "Five years. Since Mom shipped me up here to work with Uncle Felix."

"His uncle was a buddy from the service, like your dad. They both served under me. Felix came up here to fish with me after his second tour. Now he's retired in Miami with his ass on the beach while I scrape fish guts off a rusted piece of metal," he said.

"You'll still be here when *I* retire to Miami," Marco laughed.

Captain signaled me, and we left Marco on the deck, whistling and laughing to himself.

Captain gave me a tour of his thirty-foot-long boat. The stern. The cabin we'd all be sharing. The Jerk-Off Parlor, where Captain introduced me to Anna. He took his cap off in front of her and revealed his buzz-cut skull.

"She's a beauty alright, all-American. Goddamn, I love those blue eyes."

Captain was an old-fashioned pornographer. He liked his women 2-D, flat eyes on flat tear-outs. His porn was ancient, paper. Mine was modern, secrets held on the internet. The problem was I didn't clear my search history the last time I used the computer.

He never mentioned finding it, but a week after I forgot to clear "bears with big cocks" my dad said, "Before you leave for school, why don't you spend the summer in Alaska fishing with my buddy the Captain? You need the sea air. It will do you good. You don't spend enough time outdoors."

I barely slept at all the first night because I was too nervous about starting work the next day and anxious about my new surroundings. When Marco and Captain fell asleep, I slipped outside and stood on the deck. In the darkness I watched the still water, not looking for anything but wondering if there was any wildlife to see at night. If you stare long enough at the water, your eyes play tricks on you and make shapes out of the moonlight on the waves. You could go crazy staring at the water long enough, hoping to find something in it.

I puked my guts out the first week, caused by a combination of the boat's beating against the waves, like a roller-coaster drop where the boat dips down and my stomach moves in the opposite direction, and the fish—their god-forsaken smell, their wriggling bodies, their death.

By week two, I had managed to keep my insides on the inside, but I had lost weight from the previous week of puking, plus the labor that lasted from sunup until sundown and the fucking awful food Captain had for us to eat on the boat. I couldn't look at myself in the mirror anymore—I hated seeing my sunken cheeks and sunburned nose.

"I knew you'd get the seasickness under control eventually," Marco said to me one day as we hauled in a load of sockeye salmon. "It takes time, but you're tougher than you think."

"Yeah, when I started out in the navy all those years ago, I puked everything out but my balls," Captain added. "You're doing a lot better, Kevin. I was worried about you the first week because you look like one of those kids who never goes outside, spends too much time on the internet. You've proved me wrong."

I smiled and nodded. It would ruin the moment if I said "thanks."

His approval felt good, like something I wasn't used to. It was the closest I would get to earning my dad's approval. I hadn't figured out what my dad told Captain his reason was for shipping me up here. Chances were he was too embarrassed to tell Captain. Whatever my dad thought he knew about me, it didn't inspire proud-parent sharing with his navy buddies.

"I think I'll become a vegetarian as soon as I return home," I half joked with Captain and Marco.

Truth was, I was ready for a lot of changes. I looked forward to Seattle—for its art scene, other people who looked like me, and neighborhoods like Capitol Hill, places that would welcome me in more ways than my dad ever did. At school I hung out with drama club girls and other art weirdos, people who wanted to get out as bad as me.

I would have looked forward to the seafood in Seattle too if I hadn't seen the hundreds of salmon hauled in daily, flapping as they suffocated. The lucky ones were killed by the tightening net before it was pulled back onto the boat.

When I cut my hand on the net yesterday, Marco helped me bandage it. I watched his hand move over mine, and my skin flourished into dozens of goosebumps. My hands were blisters and the raw skin leftover from blisters that had already popped.

"My girlfriend Marylou's a nurse," he said as he cleaned my hand. "She's great at what she does. She does so much during these summers when I'm up here—three of them now she's put up with. She works during the day at the hospital while her mom watches our son, then she takes care of him at night. She puts up with a lot of my shit."

Marco talked. I watched his lips move—full, chapped from the rough sea air. He held my bleeding hand between both of his as he talked and wrapped. He was a decade older but looked young for his age—brown skin, shaved head, a mouth that smiled when it talked.

I often caught myself staring at Marco while he worked—it was hard to avoid it since he was one of only two humans I saw for days at a time. But it wasn't just that. It was his complete disregard for shirts on warm days and the tattoos he chose to tell his life story. His body was like a book that I read in quick glimpses—a scar on his lower right abdomen maybe from having his appendix removed, the biceps I watched him watch as he curled weights during downtime.

I felt myself growing hard from his touch. I wasn't used to being touched by anyone the way I wanted. I had one girlfriend my junior year—Julie, an artist like me. We went to homecoming and prom, and she cried on the car ride home after prom. She knew before I did.

"Did you ever get that Marylou to put on a sexy nurse's costume? I bet she'd look fine in one of those. Is she into the kinky stuff?" Captain asked Marco.

Marco dropped my hand and I took a seat, the moment over.

"She likes it a little rough, but she isn't too adventurous. I had a girlfriend once, though, who loved to dress up as a schoolgirl and strip for me first. She was one of those dirty girls who went to Catholic school."

We were cleaning up for the day. Captain traded the net for a cup of coffee with a shot of whiskey.

"Yeah, my second wife, she had a thing for doing it in places where we could get caught—the car, bathrooms at restaurants.

One time she begged me to fuck her at the zoo, in front of the otters for Christ's sake. She was a crazy bitch, that one. Better than my first wife, though, who lay there like a dead fish like she thought her job was done if she just showed up." Captain took a long drink and looked at me. My turn. "How about you, kid? You get a lot of fine young pussy down in Washington?"

"Not much. I had a girlfriend last year, but it didn't work out," I answered, hoping that would be it.

Captain leaned toward me and held his flask out to me. "No worries, kid. There's time yet for you, late bloomer. I bet you'll barely have time to study at college, you'll be buried knee-deep in pussy."

I accepted the flask and took a long swallow to avoid responding. I looked at Marco, who was nodding and smoking. He looked out at the water. The whiskey felt warm in my chest, comforting.

"You know what sirens are, kid?" Captain asked me today while we worked.

"No sir," I answered. I'd recently taken to calling him "sir." It seemed right.

"They're the creatures from Greek mythology who distracted the sailors. They were little bitches, those ones. Killed a lot of sailors."

"Were they like mermaids?" Marco asked, tossing a bad fish off the boat. I watched it fly and land with a thud onto the water. It was calm today, the sky clear enough that you could see all of the Chugach range if you had the time to look up.

"No, no. That's a common mistake. They didn't live in the water. They lived on some little island off the coast of Greece. Anyway, they'd sing and mesmerize sailors with their music. Then the sailors would either wreck their ships on the rocky coast or die other ways."

"What other ways?" I asked, in need of a distraction from tedious work—casting the net, waiting for it to fill, and hauling it back in, Captain reeling in the net and Marco and I picking the fish from the mesh.

"I don't know how to explain it—mythological ways. The men would die when the sirens' song ended. Their flesh would rot and fall off, shit like that."

"How do you know this, Captain?" Marco asked, wiping beads of sweat off his forehead with the back of his arm.

"I went to college after the war. I had vet money. I took a bunch of classes to see if anything interested me. Nothing stuck, but I always remembered learning about sirens in the introduction to Greek mythology class."

"Have you ever seen one?" I asked with a smile I kept from him. I don't believe in anything like that—mythological, supernatural, or spiritual. But I do believe sometimes people need to see something to make them feel better, a little less alone.

"Maybe. When I was young—twenty-one, twenty-two—on my first tour and off the coast of Vietnam, I thought I saw something. You spend too much time at sea and you'll see anything. But I thought it was a woman in the water. She had black hair, as dark as the water that night."

"If she was in the water, wouldn't that make her a mermaid?" Marco asked.

"You're right," Captain said thoughtfully. Then he added, "Probably for the best I didn't go after her if she was a mermaid. I don't like my women to smell fishy." He chuckled to himself.

In our cabin earlier tonight, Marco and I talked before we went to bed. Captain stayed out on the deck, finishing his nightcap.

"What did you think of Captain's story? He's full of shit most of the time, but at least he's entertaining." Marco stood by the door and pulled his shirt over his head. He stood in front of me and scratched his bare chest.

"I liked his story. Even if it ends in death, I like it. I like that the sirens gave the sailors something to distract themselves with."

"Yeah, that's a good point. Hey, you ever read any poetry? You ever read 'The Rime of the Ancient Mariner'? I like that word, 'mariner.' It's a cool way to say sailor. Anyway, that's a good poem. Pretty trippy. That Coleridge guy took a lot of opium. No wonder." Marco leaned against the wall, talked with his hands. He ran his hand indifferently over the ship tattooed across his right shoulder.

"No, I haven't read it. I haven't read a lot of poetry. I should read more," I answered sheepishly, apologetically.

"No man, it's no big deal. My mom's a high school English teacher. She kept a lot of books around the house, was a big reading pusher."

This was the moment to confide in him. No Captain. No Dad. Nobody else but Marco, whom I was hopelessly infatuated with even if he didn't feel the same or see me that way. But the door opened and Captain walked in, a rush of cold night wind following him, washing bitterly over me like sea mist.

"What are you two still doing up? This isn't a sleepover, girls. Go to bed. We have an early morning." Captain lumbered to his bed and lay down face-first.

Marco walked to our bunks and slapped me on the shoulder. "Night," he said and climbed past me to the top bunk.

The night before my flight to Alaska, silent and pissed off while I packed, Dad stood in my doorway watching me. Mom stayed downstairs in the laundry room, her unofficial sanctuary where she goes to escape mine and Dad's fighting. Dad didn't speak at first, only drank slowly from the mug of jasmine tea he had at night while reading the paper he woke up too early for in the mornings.

"Your mother babies you too much. We should have had another child. You needed a sibling, but your mother's pregnancy was difficult. I wanted you to play sports and go to camp, but she didn't like anything that might get you hurt. She *babies* you too much, her only son," he offered as explanation. I didn't know what the explanation was for: my being gay or his feeling like it was something he could have prevented. He didn't hug me goodbye.

The waves pull at me, prevent me from sleeping. It's been at least an hour since Captain passed out, a half hour since Marco fell asleep, judging by his snoring. It sounds like he's competing with the waves tonight.

I lay on my bunk staring at the bottom of Marco's bunk, knowing, feeling he's up there sleeping easily. I can't find release.

It's my mother's solemn face, my dad's silent disappointment. It's Captain's stories. It's the dead fish and seasickness and cold wind and early mornings. It's loneliness. No release. No release.

I sit up in bed and pick my shoes off the floor. Standing, I pull my sweatshirt on and creep across the room. Outside, the wind is biting. I walk to the railing and look out at the sea. Marco walks up behind me, but I don't hear him. It isn't until he puts his hand on my shoulder that I realize he's there.

"Hey, man."

"Oh hey," I say and turn back to the water.

"I heard you leave the cabin. Something wrong?" Marco asks.

"I can't sleep. Not a big deal."

We don't talk for a while, but I can sense him watching me out of the corner of his eyes.

"It's hard to adjust to sleeping out on the water like this. I haven't gotten used to the sound of the waves yet," I offer as an explanation. I grip the railing but let go, trying to relax.

He puts his forearms on the railing and leans over it. "It takes time to get used to being out here, cut off from everything. But I like it. It's good sometimes to live a solitary life. It helps you think about things. Whatever you need to sort out, you have plenty of time to think about it when you're hauling dead fish all day," he says and laughs. I can feel him giving me advice.

"I'm gay," I blurt into the darkness. My words fall from my mouth and are swallowed by the darkness below.

"Yeah, man. That's cool." He pats me on the back when he says it, a physical gesture meant to show he means it.

"You're not surprised. Is it that obvious?" I ask, suddenly insecure. We're having the conversation sideways, both looking at the water. But I turn to him now since I've already laid myself bare.

"Yes and no. I had a feeling, but I wasn't a hundred percent sure. I see the look you get when Captain talks about women, you know, kind of uncomfortable. He's harmless, by the way—just old and doesn't give a fuck about being PC."

"Why didn't you say anything to me earlier?"

"Why would I? It's not a big deal. Plus, it seems like something private to you. Why would I call you out on something you don't want to talk about?"

I could hug him I'm so thankful he said that, so thankful he doesn't care. I've never appreciated indifference more. But all I can muster is a "thanks."

"What about my dad?" I ask him, or myself.

"He'll still love you. Or he won't and you'll find love somewhere else. My dad left us when I was fifteen. He's never met my son. But what did happen was my mom became two parents.

And as soon as she saw my cousins start joining gangs or getting shipped off to juvie, she sent me up here to fish with Uncle Felix and Captain and kept me away from LA during summer break. I was pissed the first summer, of course. Now, I can't imagine a summer not spent here."

I try to picture my lips forming the words to tell my dad, but I can't quite get to the visual. Maybe when I return from fishing. Maybe after a year away at college. Someday, when I know I am ready to handle his response either way.

"So what are you doing out here anyway? Looking for sirens?" Marco asks.

"I needed the fresh air. It feels so claustrophobic in there when I can't sleep."

Marco backs away toward the cabin. "Alright, man, I'll leave you alone. I'm tired as hell. Come back to the cabin soon. If you fall off the ship and leave me out here alone with Captain, I'll jump overboard. It's been nice having someone under sixty to talk to."

"I'll come back soon. Please don't tell Captain what we talked about out here," I beg him.

"No way would I do that to you. I'm your friend. Don't worry so much. Go back to staring at the water and maybe you'll see something interesting. Every sailor needs a distraction." His laugh trails behind him as he walks away.

When I crawl back into bed, not long after Marco has returned to the cabin, I find myself more tired but still unable to sleep. I feel something different from restlessness—anticipation, maybe, of what's to come. That was the first time I ever said it out loud. The words came out so easily, like small pebbles being dropped onto still water. I stare up at Marco's bed like he's my savior, like his acceptance will get me through the rest of this summer.

My eyelids begin to feel heavy. Then Marco's arm falls down from the side of the bed, bare and dangling. I watch it tick away the minutes like a pendulum, and I feel myself relax. I think that maybe if I let it, his snoring could be like a siren song, drown out the sound of the waves, wash over me, be the death of me.

I reach out for him. Just a touch—his sea hands, his rough skin. I could die, let my skin fall away, for one touch. I touch the palm of his hand with my fingertips, a graze really. He doesn't move. I grow confident and reach for him again. For just a moment our fingertips touch and I wash away in quiet release. I am sea foam. I am peace. I am okay.

THE FIRST WIFE

Now that Tom's dead, I have to think about a lot of things. First, I think about all of his life, before, with, and after me. If I had to put the list of Tom's life in chronological order, it would go like this:

1. Birth
2. Learning to fish from his dad
3. Marrying me
4. Having the twins
5. Going to college (him, not me)
6. Getting stories published the first, second, and third time
7. Drinking all the time (the both of us)
8. Getting published more, and the teaching gig that came after
9. Meeting her
10. Losing our Tommy

11. Leaving me

12. Getting his novel published

13. Sobering up (him, not me)

14. Winning all those awards

15. Death

He led a full life, even if he constantly doubted himself as a writer. Even if we weren't the best parents in the world and even if we made some mistakes in our younger days, we always did so with pure intentions. Tom and I moved away from Yakima when he was nineteen and I was eighteen—just out of high school and a new bride, still thin as a beanpole. Sometimes those wedding pictures make me laugh; we looked like such babies then, even as I carried ours inside me. We went to California and got jobs and made lives for ourselves. We never depended on anyone else; we knew we'd only have each other in the end.

We both worked toward the same goal: make Tom a writer. Make everyone see how good his stories were. The kids, the bills, everything else came second to that. It was agreed upon on our wedding day; we both wanted it so bad it may as well have been written in our vows. Sometimes when you love someone so much, you want what's right for him more than you want what's right for you.

If I had to put the list of Tom's life in order of importance according to him, it would go like this:

1. Birth

2. Getting his novel published

3. Meeting her (sometimes I think this one swaps with the one above)

4. Sobering up

5. Learning to fish from his dad

The rest of the list fades into a blur, swirling like gray sea foam, like the kind I imagine he threw rocks in when he stood on the beach next to the house he owned (with her, not me—we never lived in a big house on the beach). The rest of the list is a jumble of words and images that mixed together in his head before he passed, when his organs clicked off one by one, when his brain was nothing left but a lump of useless tissues.

I want to tell the reporters that I know how Tom saw his life. I still understand him all these years later. This is the list I'll give to the reporter when he comes to my house to write his profile. It was years ago when news of Tom's second marriage became gossip for the *New Yorker* crowd. Nobody asked me about it. They loved how poetic it was, his marrying another writer and fellow professor. The magazines haven't published anything about his personal life in a while, but when he died of a heart attack last week, the stories started up again. It's funny, all those years spent destroying his liver and lungs with alcohol and cigarettes, and it was his heart that gave out. I always knew it was too big for one person.

There was a time—a mad time, a wild time—when we loved like the rest of the world needed it, depended on it even. There was the time at the party—with all those poets, the Vietnam protesters, and the memoirist who wrote about the Stonewall riots— and Tom and I were drinking Jameson that night. I had on my best cocktail dress (my *only* cocktail dress). It was lavender and hugged my hips that had swelled with pregnancy and never quite gone down.

This was right after he got his first story in the *New Yorker* about the young couple standing in the grocery store, fighting over which brand of toilet paper to buy. We stood in the kitchen listening to a handful of undergrads praise him for it.

"How does being a husband and father affect your writing?" one of the boys, an oily beatnik in a turtleneck, asked.

Tom was still on the verge, respected on the West Coast but only then becoming known on the East. He cleared his throat and told the kid, "Well, son, marriage isn't easy. Anyone who tells you so is a liar. But I'd be lying if I said being married to Sara Jean and raising our two kids together didn't make me a better writer and a better man."

It's funny he said that then because we were going through an especially rough patch. I had just found out he'd been sneaking behind my back with one of the other waitresses at my restaurant, and I'd begun seeing my professor—I was vaguely working toward my BA then. Most nights only one of us slept at home. At least once, neither of us made it home, but the kids were good at taking care of themselves anyway.

"You know we had that same fight when we were just a couple of years into our marriage," I told the students. "Tommy and Marianne were toddlers then, I was burnt out taking care of the kids during the day and working nights at the diner, and Tom was working on finishing his bachelor's down at Santa Barbara when it happened."

After the undergrads left, Tom turned to me and said, "Why'd you tell 'em that?"

"So what? I didn't tell them how you wanted to buy the expensive kind of paper, but I wanted to save the money. I didn't tell them when you wrote the story, you switched it around and made it so that the wife wanted the expensive kind."

He looked like he was about to say something when that student of his from the fiction class at UC Berkeley, the one wearing the paisley print dress, walked by making eyes at him.

I stood in front of him. "I typed up the first draft, Tom. Not that little slut in a skirt."

He hit me so hard, I still feel it in my neck when I turn my head too fast, like whiplash. There was blood all over the kitchen and the poor host and his wife scrambled to find a towel to hold to my nose. I bled all over her clean white dishrag. We could tell by the host's look that we weren't welcome anymore that night, so we left the party.

Tom got down on his knees in the driveway to beg my forgiveness. "I didn't mean to get mad at you, Sara Jean, I promise. I'm an oaf, and I get angry sometimes when it feels like you're trying to turn my writing on me. You can't use a man's work against him. And just because some college girl with a crush walks by me doesn't mean I'm doing anything about it. You can't go around insinuating like that."

I wiped off the little pieces of gravel stuck to his pants when he stood up. He offered to buy me a drink down the street. I still don't remember who drove, but I do remember making love to him later when we made it back to our bedroom. I remember it because some of the blood from my nose stained the shoulder of his white T-shirt, proof that my blood was a part of him. He threw the shirt out the next day; a stain like that doesn't go away.

The reporter should be here in an hour. The house is clean, but I clean it again—dust the shelves, straighten the furniture, and wipe the mirrors. My hair is still in curlers because I want it to look just right when my photograph is taken. My best tube of red lipstick is waiting on the bathroom counter so I can apply it right when the doorbell rings. It's the same shade I used to put on when Tom and I would go out dancing during our brief courtship; I'd put on a fresh coat at the end of the night and leave a big stain on his cheek when we were on the dance floor. We could dance for hours when we were kids. It was the thing I was best at besides loving Tom.

I want to set the record straight with the reporter. I don't want them referring to me as "a woman scorned." I don't want to contribute to their lies, their vicious cycle of he-said, she-said. I know Tom still loved me after our divorce took; it just wasn't in the same way anymore. He couldn't un-love me. You can't give someone nearly thirty years of your life and then make those feelings disappear just because you start to love someone else. You just have to store those first feelings in another place, like when you put your winter sweaters in a drawer once the weather begins to warm.

I never read the articles they print about Tom and that woman. I keep all of them, everything I find printed about him, organized in chronological order. But if I see her in the first photograph, dressed in cuffed jeans and oversized jackets at one of their readings or see a quote from Tom saying, "I feel I got it right this time," I stop reading. I've got folders full of the clippings from magazines and newspapers, even the article from our hometown paper when he won the National Book Award that called him "a golden boy from a stark Pacific Northwest landscape." I keep all the clippings in the extra bedroom. I have a filing cabinet as tall as me. It's got other stuff too, some of the early manuscripts I typed out for him when he'd be so full of a story that he couldn't sit still. So I'd sit still for him, picking at the typewriter while he paced the room, dictated, and chain-smoked.

I've got the newspaper clippings, the manuscripts, and of course his letters. Tom loved writing so much that when he finished a new story, he'd move on to letters to keep himself occupied. I swear, sometimes he wrote and rewrote the grocery list because he just had to take his pen to paper. Tom wrote me letters throughout our courtship, when we were married and I stayed in California with the kids the summer he taught in Oregon, even after we divorced—every once and a while, just enough to check in on my mother and me and to send a little cash over each month. When my mother died last year, Tom wrote me a beautiful condolence letter; he couldn't make it to her funeral, because he was spending the summer teaching in Europe on a fellowship, but I must have read the letter a dozen times. His last letter he wrote to me a month before he died. He knew it then, that it was coming, even if she wouldn't invite me over to say goodbye.

"I wanted to give him peace and privacy in his final days," is one of the quotes from her that appeared in the newspaper article today.

Joke's on her, really. In Tom's last letter, he sent me one hundred dollars to buy myself a new black dress and told me to come say goodbye to my "beloved oaf." "Dearest Sara Jean," the letter started—like all his others—and then, at the bottom, "It's time to say goodbye to your beloved oaf. Love, Tom."

He sent it directly to me. I put it in the box with the Christmas cards Marianne and her family send me every year. He wanted me to be a part of the end because I was part of all the rest. That's what I'll tell the reporter. I'll tell the reporter everything.

I check the clock and see the reporter is late. This one's from the *Seattle Times*. I had to call him up to offer my interview. Funny, they should be chomping at the bit, those greedy muckrakers, but nobody called when Tom died. He's probably just out of journalism school and hasn't learned professional, or common, courtesy. One of the biggest writers to come out of this region dies, you think they'd want to hear from his wife. Who do they think helped inspire those goddamn stories?

I fix myself a whiskey neat to calm my nerves. I never did grow used to talking to the reporters back when Tom and me were married. It seemed like they always wanted something from me I couldn't give them, a secret juicier than I'd ever share. Sometimes Tom and me spilled our private selves into the public, but that was at parties or bars and just because we had been drinking too much and didn't make it home in time before one of us exploded. But I never would have told the reporters about Tom's affairs. They're bloodhounds, and I won't give them the satisfaction.

We spent the summer in Mt. Shasta after our Tommy died. He was only twenty-four when the motorcycle accident happened. I got too sad after Tommy's passing. It was hard for me to shake it. Tom tried hard to make it better for us. We hid from everybody, just Tom, me, and Tom's typewriter. But I was feeling so dark then, and we both drank too hard. I knew Tom had his girl in San Francisco. At the end of the summer, he went back to her.

We talked about Tommy and Marianne on the drive back because it was easier than talking about us. The highway stretched long and forgiving, and Tom sped the whole drive home.

"Sometimes I think Tom Jr. and Marianne resented us for the way we raised them. The kids didn't get a fair shot making friends since we moved them so much," Tom confessed somewhere on the mountain pass. "We never kept them enrolled in a school for more than two years."

"I think it was good for them to have the adventure," I told him. I was an army brat myself. "Besides, by the time they were teenagers, they'd figured out that they had to take second place to your writing." I placed my hand on his shoulder and squeezed it. I was only saying what we were both thinking.

He shrugged away, unable to move more than a few inches in his seat. "I don't like hearing you say that. It makes me feel awful."

"Maybe writers shouldn't have children since the work has to be the first child."

"Maybe *we* never should have."

That might have been true, but the two of us made some mistakes in those early days and sometimes you have to take life as it comes.

"I regretted it when Marianne ran away; she was only six-teen, after all. But she seems happier in Yakima, like maybe that's where she belongs. At least I know my family's looking after her," I said, hoping that reminder would make him feel better. It's best to recognize your shortcomings; that way you can move on and focus on what you're good at.

Tom nodded but didn't speak. He fell into one of his moody silences, his "thinking silences" as I liked to call them, for nearly thirty miles.

"You understand now that this is over for good, right? This isn't like the other times. I'm not coming back. I'll be moving out of the house, moving my stuff out, and living with Janeane. I need you to tell me that you understand." I stared at his face, fatter because he had quit smoking for the third time so he had nothing to balance the eating he did when he wrote. He kept his jaw clamped tight when he was done talking. He looked like a stern father, a look I only saw in rare flashes when he dealt with the children, if he bothered to.

"I understand plenty, Tom. You found someone to go off and have your fun with. Just don't be expecting to come crawling back to me next time you need a story typed up."

"Sara Jean, I won't be coming back," he said and let out a heavy sigh. He shook his head, started looking like I how I imagined he looked when he was teaching. *Professorial* is what they call it.

"That's what you always say," I whimpered. I turned my head when I felt the tears prickling the edges of my eyes. I didn't like his talking to me like that, like I needed things explained to me twice. How many other times had he left me for those other women, only to come back when he realized they were just girls? So maybe she was his age and that was new, but that didn't mean he was. He was no different than the oaf who stumbled all over himself to ask me to dance. We were both no different. We were the same.

"I love you, Sara Jean. You're the love of my youth. But I don't want a shadow, I want flesh and blood." I don't know if he was looking at me or the road when he said it.

I kept my eyes fixed on the highway and said, "But I am flesh and blood. I'm yours."

I hear the phone ring and hurry to answer it. Maybe the reporter needs directions. My home is a little out of the way. You have to get off the ferry in Kingston and drive a ways out of town. I'm not used to giving out directions, because there's nobody to visit, but I like it better this way. It's quieter.

"Hello," I say after the second ring.

A man's voice comes through. "Yes, hi. Is this Sara?"

"Yes, this is Sara Jean." I hold the phone between my head and shoulder so I can use both my hands to fix another drink. I feel parched just talking on the phone. I don't talk to too many people these days. I quit waitressing a year ago after the sale went through on my and Tom's old house in California. I don't know if it was the land value or because Tom had owned it, but I made enough money from the property to live off. I never liked waitressing anyway; I always wanted to be a teacher, but there was never time to finish my degree.

"Hi Sara. This is Craig from the *Seattle Times*. It's about our interview." This reporter is the only one who got back to me. I left a lot of messages on answering machines this week. As he talks, I run my hand across Tom's obituary spread out on the kitchen counter. They've got a picture of him that must have been taken in the last couple of years. He's sitting at a desk with a fancy new desktop computer. He's trying to smile. "Something came up and I need to reschedule. Does next week work for you?"

I say yes of course to the reporter because I really do want to talk to him, to all of them. I want to tell the papers about Tom's love for me because the truth deserves to be told. She should know how much it was there. *I* knew it was there. It was there for twenty-five years of marriage. She only got him for five.

I should be the one to tell the reporters about Tom, but they don't see it that way. They don't realize they need me to really know him. What they want they've already got: The prolific writer killed by his own vices. The new wife left grieving. The various relatives they can dig up from up and down the West Coast to tell their "I remember Tom when" stories. A few of his contemporaries have survived—the poet who used to take salvia at Joshua Tree so he could see his poems, the raging drunk novelist nobody thought deserved the Pulitzer, and the playwright who couldn't cut it in New York so he moved to California to write for TV and support his coke habit. Maybe they'll show up at the funeral, although I doubt they would recognize me. I left the party when Tom left me. But the reporters could get some good quotes from those other writers. They'd be able to speak more eloquently than me anyway. What they don't know is that they need me. It's a human-interest piece. You can't have one of those without me.

If I had to put Tom's life in order of importance according to me, the top five would look like this:
1. Death
2. Birth
3. Marrying me
4. Getting his novel published
5. Sobering up (him, not me)

I list it like that because I see these as the events most important to Tom as a writer. Sometimes, when he was in the thick of his addiction (be it booze, pills, or the many women whose beds he shared on nights I'd kick him out of ours), he'd lose sight of the main goal. That's why sobering up was so important to keeping him going. Addiction is such a funny thing—you love one thing so much that you can't have even a little bit of it or else it'll kill you.

Many people claim his second wife was the reason he sobered up, but I think the reason was that his novel was finally published. He tasted what he could finally have—success—and he realized if he wanted to keep it, he had to get rid of the toxic stuff. Maybe she played a part, but it was small.

I put me above the others because I helped him for as long as we were together and even when we were apart. When I was a kid, my mother told me, "Sara Jean, you're going to make a man very happy someday, and it's your job to support him and put him above all else. Taking care of your family is the most important work you'll ever do." Everyone has a purpose in life, and mine was to help Tom achieve success as a writer.

Birth comes next because you can't make a great writer without starting with a man. I chose death as the most important part of Tom's life because you can't be born a great writer, but you can die one, and the dying is the part that solidifies you, moves you from man to legacy. Now Tom will no longer be the drunk who occasionally writes stories. He'll be the great writer who died too soon. I think he would have liked that.

Too bad he can't enjoy it, though. We worked so hard when we were young, but the acclaim came so late in life. Youth is wasted on the young; that's what they say. Maybe we wouldn't have known what to do with it. We got to be so good at scraping by, we probably would have thought the things that came later—the money, the recognition, the career—were all a joke.

I'd like to see Tom one more time, even if it is inside a coffin. I'd like to take the ferry out to San Juan for his funeral, even though I know she doesn't want me there. I've never been to San Juan Island, but that's where they bought their little cabin to escape to when he wasn't teaching in New York. He finally made it in the East, and all he wanted was to hide away on an island off the West Coast. I'd like to see what suit they dressed him up in because in our time, we could only afford thrift store suits that were either too short in the arms or missing a button.

I'd like to go to his funeral, walk right past her, and lean into his casket. I'd whisper, "It was the happiest for me too. I'll die now too, Tom, and that will be okay."

We were five years into our marriage when we finally found the time and a bit of extra cash to take a honeymoon. It was only for four days, and we had to beg and plead with my coworker to watch the kids for us.

We bought two bottles of champagne to drink on the drive up to Yellowstone. It was mid-August, so we camped. We didn't fight once the whole time except on the trip home over who would drive—I was tired and he was stoned. But for those nights camping under the stars, making love under the wide Montana sky, and the mornings when he fished, and the afternoon we saw the buffalo, we didn't fight; we were happy.

And Tom said, "This is the happiest I think I'll ever be in my life. I could maybe die now and that'd be okay." I didn't say anything to him then, just thought it—that I felt the same.

One more drink will keep me from shaking. It's so hard to open these pill bottles when you're jittery like this. It's hard to lay all the pills out in little rows, but that's what I do, lay them out in three neat rows on the bedside table. Sitting down on the bed, I take another drink to calm my nerves. I'm so anxious I spill some of the whiskey on my dress. But this is what I have to do; this is what's right. Tom and me until the end.

No, I should wait until next week. After I talk to the reporter. If I'm doing this, I should do it right. I've got to set the record straight before I join him. She gets a profile in the literature magazines; I get a sentence in the obituary. But I'm more than that, Tom. I'm flesh and blood.

I unscrew the bottle cap and scoop the pills back into it. I move through the house, tidying up, unable to sit still. It's hard to come down from this feeling, knowing soon everybody will know that my love was bigger. I'll tell the reporter, "What kind of wife can go on living after she loses her husband?" Would this new wife do it? Or will she go on living and writing her books and getting on without him? That's not love. Loving someone is needing them so bad that when they die, you die too. I'm your flesh and blood. I die too.

I want to think of Tom right at the end. I want to remember him when we met, when we were two small-town kids who didn't know better. I'll think of the way his mouth could never quite make a full smile, only curl to one side like he was smirking, even if he genuinely wanted to smile. I'll think of his big eyes, his "deer eyes," I used to call them, always open wide so he didn't miss anything. I'll think of him standing a foot taller than me, having to lean down in order to kiss me.

I'll close my eyes when I lay my head down on the pillow, and I'll see Tom's face at twenty, at thirty, at forty, the lines that deepened on his forehead, the creases near his mouth, the marks of age, the reminders of mortality. I'll think of him and we'll be together again—we'll be together again so soon, Tom. If he went to heaven or if he went to hell, I'll be with him first.

CLOSING JOE'S BAR

"Hello, yes, hi. I'd like to report a missing person." It was funny how you had to call the nonemergency line for something like this, funny listening to someone tell the parents of a missing person that this was a nonemergency.

"And now, you say nobody has heard from your son in two days?" The policewoman's voice over the phone was calm, soothing, like he imagined a phone-sex operator's voice would sound, not that Gary had ever called a phone-sex line before.

He nodded, then realized she couldn't see his movement and said quickly, "Yes ma'am."

"Has he ever or does your son now drink and/or use drugs?"

He knew it must have been part of the job for her to ask, but somehow it still made him feel like he had done something wrong. "Yes, to both. Alcohol mostly, but Chris's past, well, it hasn't been perfect."

"Has he ever left before? Does he have a history of leaving without notice?"

"When he was younger, in college, he'd disappear on binges every now and again, and it would be a little while until we heard from him." Gary tightened his hand around the beer he had been holding since before he dialed. He told himself he would wait until after the phone call to open it.

"Mmmhmm," she made a judgmental sound in her throat like she expected that answer. "It sounds to me like he might be on another binge. You'd be surprised how often that's the case." Now she sounded like one of those types who don't trust men, think they're up to no good.

You'd be surprised that Gary had been faithful to his wife for over twenty-five years, but that didn't mean it wasn't true.

"With all due respect, officer, it's different this time." He liked calling her "officer"; it felt funny saying it to a lady.

"How so?"

"Well see, his wife, my daughter-in-law, she's in the hospital right now. She's about to deliver his baby. He left two nights ago to get a bite to eat, knowing full well she was past her due date, and he hasn't come back since."

"Now why would your son skip out on his wife when she's in the hospital about to have his kid?"

"You got me, ma'am."

"Listen, sir, I'm going to get your report in right now and send someone out to your house for further questioning. If you can give me your location, we can get someone out in the next forty-five minutes."

He hung up the phone wishing his part were over. Kim jumped up from the kitchen table, and he knew she would make a run for the vacuum cleaner—even in times of trouble, you have to clean the house for company. Mostly he felt embarrassed about the whole mess. Even if he could never give Kim the best life, even if their house was in Shoreline and not Seattle—and maybe a little too close to Highway 99—even so, it was their house, bought and paid for, and now a cop was about to show up at his door in front of all his neighbors because his son up and disappeared right before his wife went into labor. Gary didn't think it was as bad as Chris's little wife Megan and Kim thought it was, so bad they made him call the police to file the report. Kim couldn't bear to make the phone call, and you couldn't expect Megan to do it, since her water broke this morning.

Kim paused with the vacuum. "After the police leave, we have to get to the hospital. I know Megan's parents don't want to see us right now, not since it's *our* son that did this to her, but we have to show our support to everyone, especially this baby."

The way she said, "our son," it was more like she said, "your son," like this whole thing was his fault just because he was a man too. But they both raised Chris. They may not have been able to give him much on Gary's salary, but they damn sure didn't raise him to disappear on his wife a year into their marriage, especially not *now*, with the baby about to join the world in a fatherless hospital room.

He thought the week had started off badly enough, what with the flyers showing up in the neighborhood. "Save Joe's Bar" and "Don't Let Go of a Neighborhood Treasure." Joe's Bar, the same little shit hole he had been coming to after work for fifteen years now—had it been that long? He didn't go to college, his dad was a retired bus driver, and he found out his girlfriend had one on the way—what else could Gary have done but settle down, settle into the working life? All he ever wanted was a cold beer or two after work at his favorite bar.

He had never asked for much after high school. Football had been good to him but not great. Gary had been a really great bartender when he found out Kim was pregnant, the really good kind that listened to customers like a therapist, but he quit it for the baby, found that day job driving the city bus, a different place to listen to people and all their problems. All he wanted to do was take care of Kim and Chris. He worked himself to the bone day in and day out with his "Hello" and "Goodbye" and "Do you need a transfer?" The best he could have hoped for Chris was that he'd be smart enough to get through college, wouldn't end up driving the line through the University District and have to see too many kids showing him what life could have been like if he were smarter, or luckier.

"What will it be today, Mr. Harrison?" the bartender asked when he sat on his stool. His stool: tall and mahogany, to match the bar, but a little wobbly in one leg. They never did get that fixed.

He never saw the bartender on his line, although she told him once that she was studying over at the University of Washington. She wanted to be a psychologist. That was cute, he thought, and the way she cut her hair short so she looked like a Chinese Peter Pan and covered her arms with tattoos. Becky was a lesbian, she had told him more than once, one of those hip kinds that smoked more than he did—very popular among this generation below him.

He had nothing against her kind. He respected a person's right to live their lives, but he was curious about her. Maybe she was one of those experimental college girls who rebelled too young against her parents. He'd heard that Asian parents were strict. Becky must have been a real disgrace to her family. Maybe they didn't even stay in touch with her. Some families do that. Turn their backs on their kin.

"The usual, Becky. You know some things never change," he said.

"Some things do. I know you know that from the look on your face," she said and placed the cold glass on the counter, not spilling one bit of foam as she pushed it toward him. He didn't know what to make of her, but she poured a beer better than most.

"You mean this," he said and laid a flyer on the counter. He tore it off a telephone pole on his way in, little bits of tape on the corners left as evidence. "Do you want to explain?"

"Don't give me that tone. You know as well as anyone I can't afford to be out of a job. This job may not be glamorous, but it sure as hell pays the bills."

"Well, who should I ask? Joe?" For the last year and a half that Becky had been his bartender, after Fat Tony died of a heart attack and Louis moved to the East Coast nearly a decade ago, Gary gave it away that he had had one too many if he asked who Joe really was. It didn't happen often, because he was a father after all, but when it did she told him Joe had been a cowboy or a bullfighter or a boxer long before opening Joe's Bar. Gary didn't think anyone knew Joe or that there was even a Joe to know, but he figured that if someone did, it had to be the bartender. It must have been a secret they told them in training.

"There's nobody to ask, Mr. Harrison. The lease ends in a week and patrons can rally all they want, but this neighborhood is changing. The landlord wants us out, and he raised the rent to make it happen. This place is a little too blue-collar for the condos down the street. He wants something more upscale."

After three more beers, Gary told Becky, "I want Joe to fix this."

"You know Joe can't do that, Mr. Harrison. He died in the space shuttle back in '86, just after launch. He should have stuck with bartending, I guess."

That was just five days ago, a regular Monday. Now it was a Friday, and he was about to be a grandpa, and his only son was gone. Joe's Bar was only a fifteen-minute drive, but Kim wouldn't let him go, not with the police on their way. Instead, he cracked another can and let the bubbles settle his stomach. The vacuum whooshed around the house right up until the doorbell rang. Kim hid upstairs the whole twenty minutes the officer sat in the living room with Gary. He forgot to throw out the beer before opening the door, but didn't want to ditch it with the officer inside—he didn't like the way they made him feel guilty when he didn't even do anything. Instead, he held it self-consciously on his knee as he described Chris's height, eye color, and visible tattoos or scars.

He forgot about the little one above his eyebrow, the one he gave Chris when he was sixteen and got caught stealing liquor from a convenience store. That was the last time they had fought like that, in the kitchen, with fists, and Kim had said, "I refuse to stand between you two anymore. Just go ahead and kill each other." They did stop, both out of equal dependence on the woman. And for all her talk about women's lib and going out and getting that part-time job at the library, Gary knew she needed them too, her boys. That's the thing about family: you need them more than you want them.

When Gary and Kim arrived at the maternity ward an hour later, they found out there was another little boy in their world: a son, a grandson. Even though Megan's parents excused themselves from the room as soon as he and Kim showed up, he didn't let that spoil it for him, holding this little boy like he had held Chris twenty-five years ago. And he thought that if Chris could just hold this baby, he would know what it felt like to be a father, to want to stop living your life because you have to live for this kid now.

He and Kim were shunned from the hospital when visiting hours ended. She didn't want to go home, so she made plans to have dinner with her sister. "Why don't you go to Joe's tonight, Gary? You need to get out of the house too, and it's closing soon, isn't it?"

When he arrived at the bar it was still early enough to beat the Friday-night crowd, the younger kids who thought bars like this were ironic. He thought maybe he could give one of his buddies from work a call, but he didn't know if anyone could leave home on short notice. It gets harder to get away as you get older; things pile up. So it was just Becky and him. She had to put up with him because he was a regular.

"You've got three days before this place closes, Mr. Harrison. Feel like trying something new?"

"No, Becky. I've had enough excitement today. Just give me a Budweiser."

"What kind of excitement does a man like you have?"

He told her about Chris; one, to make her feel guilty, and two, because every customer at a bar needs someone to talk to.

"I'm really sorry to hear that. How's the baby doing?"

"He's great, you know, as far as babies go. Healthy and happy, it seems. Not a care in the world."

"You've got to try your best to think of that."

"You mean instead of that little shit son of mine?"

"Be careful what you say. At least wait until you know he's alright before you hate him." Now he felt guilty, that twinge in the chest that maybe his son had died before him. What's a parent to do without a son?

At home he found Kim crying on the phone with Megan. Still no word from Chris, and Megan was cleared to leave the hospital in the morning. All these people lined up in his world—women mostly, with their tears and the way they look at you like maybe you've made one too many wrong choices in life. All these peo-ple, and he didn't know how to fix a single one of them. How could Chris do this? How could he be so selfish? He left this messy trail, and Gary was stuck cleaning up after him. That's the part of parenting nobody tells you about: the moment your kid lets you down. Gary threw a chair at the wall that wouldn't get picked up for days. There was nothing else to do but wait.

On Saturday Gary and Kim were allowed over to Chris and Megan's apartment. Her parents were conveniently out grocery shopping while the guilty parents stopped by. They had to take the blame. Without Chris around, there was nobody else. The baby slept, nameless, while Gary and Kim watched Megan tee-ter around the small apartment unpacking and tidying things up.

"We just want to say that we're really sorry, Megan," Gary said, like they had practiced in the car ride over. "We didn't see a thing like this coming."

"I suppose you never do. It always looks a little different from the outside," she said. Her eyes were sort of glassy, empty. She had the look of a new mother who hadn't slept in days.

He wanted badly to ask for more. Was there something that made Chris leave? Gary had entertained the idea before. What husband hadn't? But you don't do it when there's a kid involved. Maybe Megan told Kim the real reason on the phone, but nei-ther looked like they planned to tell him.

Megan glowed with that kind of beauty mothers get. Gary re-membered when Kim had it, that heat that radiated from her, a creator. They always talked about having another, giving Chris a little brother or sister. But Kim's pregnancy had been harder; the second time, it didn't stick. So they put it all on Chris.

After the apartment and seeing that baby asleep in the bassinet, oblivious, Gary needed to have a drink.

"Any word from the kid?" Becky asked, beer glass in hand.

"Not a syllable."

Gary had never seen the Saturday crowd before. He was a workweek drinker. They were mostly younger, still looked fresh out of college, frightened and prematurely haggard. He didn't remember looking that way at twenty-two. His generation, they took life as it came to them, didn't expect much more than what they could work for. These kids today, they expected the world to be handed to them on a silver platter—and ran away if it wasn't.

Gary drank too much that night, didn't want to face Kim at home, not with her so sad that maybe she failed as a mother, not wanting to show his stupid drunken face like he had so many times before. How many times had Kim helped him into bed, tucked him under the covers like her own son? Did she ever tell him to say his prayers? No, he must have overheard her saying that to Chris. These mothers, so protective of their boys.

"Maybe it's time you called it a night, Mr. Harrison," Becky suggested in that soft voice she put on when she needed to calm a man, calm Gary at least. Did he look that drunk?

"Maybe you should call it a night, Becky. Why don't you let me take you home tonight? Joe's Bar is closing—what've you got to lose?"

"My self-respect, Mr. Harrison. And you could lose your wife for saying something like that. Go home. She needs you now."

"But what about what I need? Nobody ever thought of that. My son ditches and leaves these women for me to deal with on my own. Maybe I should run too." All he ever wanted was a place of his own. "Now that the bar's closing, it doesn't feel like there's much reason to stay."

She breathed out heavily, a big sigh of frustration. "It's just a bar."

"When you get to be my age, Becky, it's everything."

She shouted last call to the bar. When he turned around, most of them had already cleared out.

"Go back to your mothers, children. They'll protect you," he thought.

Gary turned back to the bar. "Where are your parents? Do they live here in this country?"

"They live right here in Seattle, where they were born. I'm second generation Chinese-American. What did you think?"

"I thought," he started, but didn't know what he meant to say. Chris was always getting after him about it, always embarrassed Gary would say the wrong thing to Megan, confuse her for Mexican when she was Puerto Rican. It got so hard sometimes keeping track of things like that. When he'd grown up—down in Issaquah—everybody was the same. Now he had to watch everything he said. It got to be that you couldn't ask someone a simple question without getting in trouble.

"Tell me, Becky—who was Joe? And you better make it pretty damn good this time or else no tip." He meant it to be funny, their last laugh. He didn't want to be one of those old men who cry at bars.

She set the glass she was cleaning down on the bar. "You know, Gary, here's a little secret for you. It wasn't ever Joe at all. It was Jo without the *e*, and she was the meanest dyke you ever saw. I'm talking part truck driver, part women's soccer. She added the *e* when she opened the bar so that long after her death she could really stick it to jerks like you. And forty-six years of business later, here you are drinking it to the ground."

"That's not true, Becky. You know it," he said and smiled. He wished he could have had a daughter.

"But does it make it any easier to let it go?" she asked.

He didn't answer. He felt stupid for needing her.

"This place isn't a church. It's not a sanctuary. It's a bar. I'm sure there'll be a new one in its place in a month."

That wasn't the point, and she was too young to understand that. Everything was changing around him, slipping away. She saw him as some pathetic old man with nothing better to do. Nowhere better to be. She didn't understand that sometimes you need to get away. You need to have something constant in your life.

A cute blonde in a tight dress sat down at the empty barstool two away from Gary. She was the kind of girl a man his age could look at and get away with it: she was used to everybody looking at her, and he was past the age of registering on her radar. She looked in his direction and smiled like he was her grandfather.

"Excuse me," Becky said and threw the towel onto the bar and turned away, sort of dramatic like Gary had seen in those soapy ten o'clock dramas Kim liked to watch so much. He laughed to himself. Who needs to watch it on television when you've got enough of it to deal with right at home?

Gary watched Becky move over to the new girl, ready to take her order. Instead she said, "Hey babe, I'm off in twenty. Do you want anything while you wait?"

"No, I'm fine. Are you too tired to go out tonight?" the blonde asked her. "I know we need to get up early to make brunch with your parents."

"I wouldn't mind us going back home and watching a movie," Becky said and held the girl's hands in hers in a way Gary felt embarrassed to watch.

His glass of beer slipped out of his hand, and if it weren't for his just barely holding it above the bar, it would have shattered right there in front of Becky. He had enough trouble getting by with this crowd around him getting younger and younger. He didn't need to start dropping things on top of it.

Fifteen years coming to this place and this was how it would end: his jackass of a son doing God knows what out there, while that pretty young wife of his, all waif-like and tired and in need of care after childbirth, waited for him at home, and she probably wouldn't even hold it against him, this little spree; Kim at home falling asleep sitting up in bed, a beauty magazine strewn across her chest like she thought an article on the top ten butt-firming exercises would reverse time; and him, sitting alone at the bar while the prettiest thing he ever saw in a dress took home Becky, his girl.

He put a bigger tip on the counter than usual, at the end of a long run, when it counted, and asked Becky where she planned on going next.

She walked slowly, running a towel along the top of the bar as she moved toward him. "Well, I'm not done yet. Still have another year before I earn my degree. But I have a job lined up at a bar on Capitol Hill."

"Over there, huh? Like one of those gay bars?"

"Yes, Mr. Harrison. One of *those*."

He collected his keys and stood up. "Thanks for everything, Becky. See you around."

"Take care, Mr. Harrison."

Their goodbye that night felt like a real goodbye, and even though he didn't go to the bar on Sundays (the Lord's day, after all), he thought maybe he could swing by for one last drink after work on Monday, closing day. He wanted to avoid any of the noise and sentimentality of Joe's closing, but at five o'clock on Monday and nearing a week since Chris's disappearance, Gary couldn't find a reason to go home.

But then his cell phone rang on the drive home from work, and it was Kim, and she said, "Chris called Megan. He's done. He needs a ride. Megan can't do it, not with the baby, and God knows I can't do it."

He would forgive Chris eventually. That went without saying. People make mistakes—kids and husbands. But he also knew that if he were to ever resent Chris for anything, it would be that he called home on Monday and not Tuesday.

When he picked him up, Chris smelled like body odor and cologne, awful like he hadn't showered in a week, and he had on the same clothes he left wearing.

"What in God's name were you thinking?"

"I wasn't thinking that much. I just needed to get out. It was all closing in on me—Megan, and the baby coming—and I got scared. I didn't do much, I swear, just called up a few old friends from school and went to a few parties."

"Went to a few parties? For five goddamn days? She had the baby, Chris—do you even care?"

"Yeah, Dad, I do. That's why I need to get home. My son needs a name. She wouldn't do it without me."

"For the life of me, Chris, I'll never understand how you could do this." He kept his hands gripped on the steering wheel, his eyes on the road. You can't look at a person the same after they've let you down.

Chris pulled at his seat belt. "You must know what I felt. You've been through the same thing, not knowing what's coming, feeling like you have no say in your own life. It's not like I didn't want it. I do. It's just that there was this moment where I was sitting with Megan on the couch and she was talking about when the baby comes, and I thought, 'This is the last moment I have before it changes, before it's not just my life anymore.' Do you know what I mean?"

"Yeah, sure, I remember that feeling." When Chris was born, it felt like his whole life had stopped and started at the same time. "But the difference," he said, "was that I didn't run."

Chris didn't respond. He looked too tired to disagree. Gary drove in silence. Maybe he did run, in a way.

When he parked the car in front of the apartment building, he got out and stood in front of Chris. Chris stepped onto the curb—never quite as tall as his dad. Gary didn't know whether to shake his hand or hug him, thankful he was home but mad as hell for his leaving in the first place. Chris moved first, put his arms around Gary's shoulders. What could he do but hug him back? He had to hug him, his only son.

The bar closed down, even with all the thoughtful flyers posted around the neighborhood and the local news coverage. It became another memory, like Gary suspected he would someday. They opened up a restaurant in the space, some fancy place with regional cheese plates and twenty-five-dollar pieces of salmon, the type of place Kim dropped hints about before their anniversary. Even if the restaurant couldn't hold a candle to a good steakhouse, or even if someday it turned into a coffee house with art on its walls that would never sell, the bar would still be gone. Forgotten.

It was gone, but what could he do? The world still had to spin.

FATHER AND DAUGHTER

They drive silently to the casino. It's the old pickup her father's had since she was little—the blue Ford with the tires so tall he used to have to help her climb into the cab. He keeps the windows cracked as they drive past the mint fields on Highway 97, their crisp green smell hitting them in waves. At eighteen, her legs are long and thin, and her toes touch the windshield when she rests her feet on the dashboard. When the truck was new, he used to yell at her for putting her feet up. Now that the truck's ignition can be started without a key, he wears its oldness as a badge of honor, something that's outlasted most other things in his life. Someone with large, loopy handwriting has written, "Wash me," on the passenger-side door.

She notices the parking lot first, full for a Tuesday night. She's been at her father's apartment on Yakima Avenue since Sunday night. When she washed her hair in his shower the first morning, she found his shampoo bottle empty. She hasn't seen him since spring break three months back. He looks about the same, only skinnier. She knows that when she calls her mom tomorrow, she'll ask how he looks because her mom believes that's the marker of how the rest of his life is going. She won't mention that he's smoking more.

"Here we are, Baby Girl," he says and parks the truck. The lights of Legends Casino are red and intimidating. She thinks they should be green and more inviting, but she figures most people who come here walk right past the front entrance without looking up. "Smile," he says and reaches for her chin.

She opens the door and breathes out, mixing her exhalation with the mint-tinged night. With a small leap, she hits the ground, catching her sneakers on the gravel. Her father puts his arm around her as they cross the parking lot. He's fumbling with the pack of cigarettes in his pocket as she stares at the murals of snow-covered mountains covering the front of the building. In the summer, her family used to spread a blanket in the field behind the casino alongside other families to watch the fireworks. She misses those lights as her memory is replaced with the too-bright fluorescence of the inside of the casino. They pass the gift shop and the security guards and hover for a moment beside the tables.

Spanish 21. Texas Hold 'Em. Blackjack. Baccarat. She has a vague understanding of most of what she sees, but the environment is foreign to her, like she's dreaming. The cigarette smoke swirling through the air makes her feel hazy. "What will it be?" he asks as he too scans the room.

"I don't know. You decide."

"No, not me. We came here for you. A past-due birthday celebration. This is your night."

"Okay, how about blackjack?" She remembers friends playing it around her dorm. They'd come to her door asking her to join, but she said no, come back if they wanted to watch a movie.

"That's my girl," he says and coughs into the crook of his elbow. "I see an empty table at the back. We'll steer clear of the action for a while until you understand the rules a little better."

They walk past rows of slot machines, all colors and silly cartoons of women wearing little clothing. One cluster of machines promises a baby-blue Camaro to its lucky winner. The car shines under the casino lights. She doesn't make eye contact with the people sitting at the machines; they don't look at her. The casino is one main room with little alcoves where the poker tables and the keno areas are set up. The sounds of muffled talking, quarters clinking into buckets, and cards being shuffled are harmonious—if she closes her eyes.

"Here, this one looks good," he says and guides her to a table where a middle-aged man with a face of cascading, milky wrinkles waits for them. Her father puts his hand on her back as she sits and then sits beside her.

She looks between the two men—her father and the dealer—and sees recognition in their eyes. "How are you doing tonight, sir?" the dealer asks.

"Great. Just great. This is my daughter. She's staying for a week on her summer break from college," he says, and with a smile and a hand up to shield his mouth he adds, "Couldn't get the ex to let me have her for longer. But you know how that is."

She leans in to read the dealer's nametag—Mitch—and nods a hello. "I've never played before. I don't think I'll be any good at it."

"Are you kidding me? It's all about beginner's luck. You'll do just fine," Mitch assures her.

"It's true. Beginner's luck is the best luck to have. That's why I haven't had a good hand of cards in twenty-five years," her father jokes. Mitch chuckles and looks at her.

Her dad lays a stack of bills on the table, but she doesn't keep her eyes on them long enough to count how much.

"Cashing in one hundred," Mitch yells to somebody, but she's not sure who.

Her dad pushes a stack of one-dollar chips toward her. She reads the sign on the table that says the minimum buy-in is five dollars.

"Will you start without me? I'd like to watch you first before I try it."

"Sure. You can watch your old man. Watch and learn."

Mitch deals a hand. Her father has a six and a ten and Mitch shows a seven. He flashes a familiar smile to her father and says, "She may watch, but I'm not sure how much she'll learn from her old man."

He waves Mitch's jab away. "First rule of blackjack: always assume the dealer has a ten for his other card. Now since he has a seven showing, I have to assume he's got me beat with seventeen. That's why I'll take another card." He hits the table with a rapid tap, the silent code between player and dealer. Mitch flips a nine.

"Bust." With a quick sweep, her father's five-dollar chip vanishes. He quickly replaces it.

"Let's see what Mitch would've had." Mitch flips his other card over and reveals a ten. "See, I had to try. It's better to bust than to let them beat you, at least that's what I always say."

She swallows at his advice. Her mouth has quickly become dry in the casino. It's not the cigarette smoke that bothers her as much as the recirculated air. She should be used to this feeling. Summers in Central Washington always get up to one hundred degrees of stale heat, but the air is different in here, unnatural.

Her father wins on the next hand after staying at nineteen. "I'd have to be crazy or drunk to go for another card on nineteen. And unfortunately, they don't serve alcohol here. So it's only my job to stay sane," he says with a laugh. He's always laughing around her. Even in her memories, before her parents split and she moved with her mom to Spokane, she remembers him laughing at the dinner table.

"Why can't they serve alcohol here? Don't the casinos want the customers drunk so they'll play more?" she asks.

"Because of the rez," Mitch answers with some disdain in his voice. "The Yakama Nation banned it. Keeps getting their people in trouble. Some people don't know when to quit."

"You gotta go into Yakima to get a cold beer at the casino. Here all you can do is smoke. It's a shame; I have better luck after a drink," her father says without looking up from his cards.

As Mitch deals the next hand, she lets her eyes wander around the room. It is full of mostly Native Americans, almost entirely men. Growing up in Yakima, the history of the area was reduced to a short unit in her fifth-grade social studies class, culminating in group projects reporting on an assigned tribe. She knows that every town name in the area—Zillah, Toppenish, Wapato—is of Native American descent, but she can't remember anything more.

She doesn't know anyone who has ever won a jackpot at Legends, least of all her father. A man with long braids catches her staring, and she flushes in embarrassment. Her skin goosebumps, and she wishes she didn't wear her cutoff shorts. She must be the youngest person in the room.

"So where do you go to school?" Mitch asks her, and she returns her eyes to the table. Her father's stack of five-dollar chips has lowered.

"Whitworth. My mom lives in Spokane, so that makes it easy for me. Plus, I got in on a scholarship."

He squeezes her shoulder. "Fancy private school. My girl's a real brain. What's that you were telling me at dinner last night about your psych class? Something about training dogs."

"I took an introduction to psychology class. We spent a week on Ivan Pavlov. He performed all these experiments on dogs and related them to humans. It's all about conditioning the dogs by giving them rewards."

"What I want to know about is if she has a boyfriend. She won't tell me that stuff. She only wants to talk about the dogs."

She blushes and watches Mitch end the hand with his black-jack. "My boy just started school too. He's over at Eastern taking philosophy and English courses. All kinds of stuff. He really likes it too. It's good for you kids to keep your education going like this. In my day, we were happy to make it out the other end of high school. Now my son tells me he wants to be a lawyer."

"I know what you mean, Mitch. I've spent my life working on houses, working with my hands, and now I've got a little girl who wants to teach. I guess she got all the brains in the family."

On the next hand, her dad lays a second chip down on his eleven and tells her this move is called a "double-down." Mitch turns over a five and then beats her dad's hand with a twenty.

"Shit," her dad says. He flicks the small pile of his remaining chips over and says, "We're moving on, Mitch. You just weren't on my side tonight, buddy."

"See you around. And good luck with school," he says with a nod to her.

She follows behind her dad as he moves from table to table, hovering behind groups and peeking over shoulders. "We can get you started at the three-dollar table if you want. That will be an easier introduction for you, and less expensive for me," he says with an elbow to her side. "Oh shit, they're all full, except that one has a spot open."

"You keep playing. I'll stand behind you and watch," she says as they move toward the table.

"Don't you want to play? That's what I brought you here for. I wanted to be the first one to take you gambling."

"I know, Dad, thanks. It's just that I don't want to lose all your money. I'm not any good at this stuff and I feel bad throwing your money away."

He stops and grabs her wrist. "Did you tell your mother? Is that why you're saying that? What did she tell you?"

"No, I didn't tell Mom we were coming here. I just feel bad, that's all. I don't want to lose what's yours."

"Don't think of it that way, kiddo." He lets go of her wrist and rubs his hand up and down her arm. "It's not about the money tonight. We're having fun, playing around. If you feel bad it takes all the fun out of it."

"Okay, you play this round. I'll jump in when a spot opens up."

They join the other players at the table. The dealer this time is a woman, round and bulging. She has swept her pale blonde hair into a loose ponytail and the shorter hairs fall in wisps around her face. She keeps blowing at them as she deals.

The dealer, Janice, is in the middle of a conversation with one of the other players when her father joins the hand. "This week off was worthless. We wanted to go camping and couldn't because we didn't have the money. Then we had the brilliant idea to have a garage sale to pay for the camping trip. After spending two bucks on the permit, we only made ten dollars. I finally just let the kids pitch a tent in the backyard so they'd quit complaining."

Her father stays on his first hand and matches the dealer, earning nothing but losing nothing. He loses two hands and then hits a blackjack on the next. He doubles his bet before busting on the next hand. As he plays, he talks to her over his shoulder about the odds in each hand. The dealer smiles as she looks between father and daughter.

She leans down to her father. "I'm thirsty. Could I get some water?"

"Sure, sure. The drink girl should be around soon. They've got to make their tips. I'll flag her down when I see her. I could use a Coke anyway."

Her sunburned chest itches. She scratches her short nails across the red skin and picks up small flakes. She idly runs her hands over her collarbones and moves her gaze around the room again. Her father talks to her about the hand he just won, but she doesn't hear him. From somewhere behind, a man asks her father if she's his "lucky charm," and he shrugs the question away.

Her eyes catch on a man playing roulette two tables away. He looks older than her father, about sixty—in the weathered skin, not his shiny black hair. He wears a leather vest over his flannel shirt like many of the other men in the casino, but he stands out from the rest of the gamblers. He has no mouth. It's like the lips were pulled away. It's just an opening, loose and fleshy. She can't stop staring, and she knows he'll look up eventually and see her. Her eyes trace the edges of the opening, the deep black cave. It looks like he could open wide and swallow all the darkness waiting outside, beyond the bright lights and flashing hope of the slot machines. He smacks the thin skin together as he lays his bet on the table, not seeing her.

She takes one more look at him and whispers to her father that she's going to find a drinking fountain.

"Alright," he says, "but you have to play when you get back. No more excuses."

She walks past the tables and the slot machines back to the entrance. Outside, the night air hasn't cooled enough for her to need her jacket, but she wraps her arms around herself anyway.

She thinks she'll count to ten before she goes back in there, but she gets to twenty and doesn't move. She wishes it were colder so she could shiver. It feels like something is building inside her, but she doesn't know if it's going to come out.

There is nothing here for her outside but the darkness, a parking lot full of pickups but nobody in sight. She won't go back in there, even if the lights flicker like a circus and the dealers welcome her with their smiles. She never should have come here. Her mom warned her not to expect anything to be different with him. She has plenty of other friends with long-gone parents, but maybe it's worse that he's still around but refuses to change. She'll stay out here and see how long it takes him to realize she left. She has to believe that this time she'll be lucky; it can't happen if you don't believe it will.

She was ten when her dad first brought her to Legends Casino. She couldn't come in because she was just a kid, and even though she begged him to let her stay at home while her mom was at work, he said it wouldn't be right to leave her there. She had told him she would get bored waiting in the truck, but he didn't listen.

"Wait here for Daddy. You've got your book, right? Just read that while Daddy plays a bit. I'll be out before chapter two."

"Okay," was all she could manage to get out. She wanted to tell him she was scared to be left alone, but she hated disappointing him. She didn't want to complain like Mom did because it made him sad.

"Remember our deal not to tell Mom about this one. She never likes Daddy to have any fun, so we have to keep this a secret." They pinkie swore and he kissed her forehead, and even though she knew she shouldn't keep a secret from her mom, she basked in the warmth of sharing it with him.

He left the windows lowered halfway, enough that she could lay her arms across the glass and rest her head on the top of her hands if she wanted to. She read three chapters before looking up to watch the sun lower behind the hills. It was a weekday, and the parking lot was crowded. She turned her book over in her hands, spinning it until it fell on the floor. She ducked when people walked near the truck, worried she would get in trouble just for being close to the casino. In the rearview mirror, she looked at the new haircut her mom had given her the week before. It made her look like a tomboy, and she feared the teasing from the boys at school.

She looked out at the fireworks field. She closed her eyes and pressed on her eyelids until she saw colors. Lying sideways on the bucket seat, she fell asleep. When she woke, the air had cooled and the only lights left came from Legends. In her dad's glove compartment, she couldn't find his watch. It was empty except for half a pack of cigarettes. She rolled one in her hand and looked at herself in the mirror. She scrunched her face to mimic her dad's and held the cigarette in her mouth. She moved the cigarette in and out of her mouth, pretending.

Outside the truck, she could hear a group of men laughing and yelling as they walked into the casino. The security guard stood out front smoking. He could probably help her, but her dad told her to stay put. She leaned her body out the window and dangled her limp arms like she was dead. Her head sank down and she felt the blood rushing to it.

The air smelled like mint, not like the chewing gum kind or that peppermint oil her mom sometimes wore. It was fresher, still rooted in the earth. It moved toward her slowly from the fields; then it rushed at her, flooding her nostrils as she perked her head up and sniffed at the air. The memory hit her all at once: her daddy folding bills and shoving them into his pockets, singing along to the radio as they drove away from home, telling her the air smelled like good luck tonight.

MOM AND THE BEAR

When I overhear Mom and her new boyfriend Ted fight, it sounds like this:

He says something real stupid like, "I wish you would control that goddamn daughter of yours."

And then Mom acts all offended like, "What do you mean? She's only twelve, for Christ's sake."

And then their voices start to overlap:

"She's always walking around the house in those cutoff shorts. Who does she think she is, Daisy Duke? Do you know what the boys around the neighborhood are going to think about her if she keeps dressing like that? Tell her to put some pants on."

"She's a child. She's not doing anybody any harm. That's just what she likes to play in." "Well, it bothers me. I wish you would control your kids better. You're their mother, Sandra, not their best friend." "Don't give me parenting advice like you're a better parent than me, Ted." "I'm a great goddamn father." "Maybe to your children. Mine seem to disgust you, and you barely have to be around them."

"I'm around them plenty, thank you. I listen to their whining and crying and bitching. Ican'ttakeitanymore. I'mnottheirdad." "ThankGodyou'renottheirdad." "Don'tyousaythattome,Sandra. Don'tyoutalkdowntome.""Maybeyoushouldgohometoyourkids andyourwife.""Don'tbringthemintothis.JustbecauseI'mnotagre athusbanddoesn'tmeanI'mnotagreatdad."

And then it just goes on *forever* and it doesn't even sound like words anymore, not even like English, just like they're squawking in some awful adult language I don't understand.

So that's what I hear all the time. I wish Mom didn't have another boyfriend. I wish she'd never met Ted, that he'd never come to get his teeth cleaned at the dentist's office where she works. She's too friendly. I don't know why dental hygienists have to be so friendly anyway. Nobody wants to be friends with the person who stabs at their teeth with those awful torture tools. Plus, they always talk to you and ask you dumb questions when they have their hands jammed down your throat. And they're always telling you to open your mouth wider. What do they want to do, see if they can shove their whole fist in your mouth?

So anyway, Mom cleaned his teeth and I guess he thought she looked pretty in those pink scrubs she has to wear, and maybe that blinding light they shine in your face at dentists' offices was romantic to Ted, because after Mom cleaned his teeth and made him swish that mouthwash stuff that always makes my mouth burn, he asked her out. So that's how she got to be dating him. And that was six months ago. Now he practically lives with us, but just at night. And I don't like having him around. He talks down to me just because I'm twelve. It's like he thinks he's my dad or something. He's *not* my dad.

Not like I know where my dad is or anything. Mom says I'm better off not knowing, but sometimes I think she must hide cards and letters from him. I bet he didn't forget my birthday this year. How could you forget a big one like a twelfth birthday? I bet he sent some really nice card and it probably had birthday cash or a gift card inside, and Mom probably hid it from me because she wants me to hate him because she hates him so much. I hate him most of the time; he left Mom and me so I kind of have to. But I don't always want to hate him. Maybe he had a good reason for leaving and just because he left doesn't mean he won't come back, even if Mom says, "You should learn while you're young to quit having faith in him—and all men for that matter."

I definitely don't want to hate him just because Mom does. I don't like doing everything she wants, and just because she hates somebody doesn't mean I have to hate somebody. If it were that way, I'd have to like everybody she likes, and then I'd have to like Ted. And I don't.

Sometimes Mom stares at the clock a lot when she's waiting for Ted to come over. I ask her why she has to wait up so late for him and she says things like, "Ted's a busy man, Lo. He has other obligations he has to deal with before he can come over."

Mom always talks about Ted's life away from her as his "obligations." I'm not a little kid, and no matter what Mom wants to call it, I know Ted's got a family, like his real family. Mom never thinks I hear anything, but they don't talk *that* quiet and from my bedroom I can hear what they say in the living room. Mom says words like "frustrated" and "used" and Ted says things like "have patience" and "we can't separate right before Leslie's sweet sixteen."

Ted's not Mom's first boyfriend since Dad left. There was the mechanic with the mean temper. The night she threw him out, she called her girlfriend Betsy over and she spent the whole night with us. A guy from work came over once, and the next night I listened in the hallway when Mom talked on the phone with her sister and whispered, "Never shit where you eat. You'd think I would have learned that by now." My half-brother Randy's dad was nice and he treated me like I was his too, and I thought maybe he would be my new dad, but he said he didn't know why he had to get married to be our dad, and then he didn't know why he had to live with us to be our dad, and then he stopped coming around. I liked the marine. He was nice and played catch with me, but he had to ship off back to Iraq, and after he left, Mom would get upset if I ever tried to ask about him.

Right before Ted there was another boyfriend. One night, he kept his hand on my lower back the whole time we watched that rerun of *I Love Lucy* while Mom was in the kitchen washing dishes. I felt the heat of his palm against my sticky back, resting on the space between the bottom of my tank top and the top of my shorts. Mom walked into the living room and saw him pull his hand off me and set it on the back of the couch. He did it really fast and then he muttered something and walked to the bathroom. My mom followed after him and a few minutes later he walked out with his head down. I crept closer to the front door and listened to Mom say goodbye to him.

"I swear to God, if you come near this house or my child again, I'll pull out my father's hunting rifle and make you regret it."

Mom would never let me see the gun. She said she had it from when she used to go hunting with her dad, but that it wasn't a toy and I should never think of it that way. The time she threatened that creep was the only time I heard her talk about it.

Mom has this funny thing she always does with Randy and me. She smells us. I don't mean like she sniffs us from head to toe.

No, it's always just the tops of our heads, like she's a mother bird smelling her baby.

I could feel Mom breathing in the smell of my hair last month when she was helping me get dressed for my first school dance. It wasn't a big deal or anything, not like a dance where you have a date. Those come later in junior high. They called it the Spring Fling and it was in the evening, not like the socials we used to have after school in fifth grade. Mom bought me a new dress. I got to pick it out, but she still had final say. Ted was there that night and Mom made me spin in my dress for him and she said, "Doesn't she look like a princess?" but Ted only made a sort of grunting sound and then went back to reading the paper. Later I heard him tell Mom, "It's not something I'd let Leslie wear."

Anyway, when she was curling my hair Mom told me I was losing my scent and I didn't know what she was talking about because it had been a while since we had talked about that.

"What scent, Mom?"

"Your baby scent. It's going away. Oh Lo, soon you'll smell like perfume and sweat, like a teenager." She got all teary-eyed then and it was really embarrassing, even if it was just the two of us. I made her leave my room so I could finish getting ready, and after she was gone I checked under my armpits to see if I smelled like a teenager yet. "At least I still have your brother," Mom had called from the hallway.

Randy and I are kind of close since we're half related and because both of us know what it's like to only have a mom stick around. But he's practically still a toddler, so it's not like I can talk to him about it. He doesn't really get it that his dad is gone, if he even remembers him. But I wouldn't tell him that. I don't want to make him sad. He's all the family I've got besides Mom. Randy will turn four this year. Mom still rubs baby lotion all over him, but sometimes he throws a fit about it and yells, "I'm a big boy now!"

Whenever he cries like that when Ted's around, Ted complains to Mom, "When my Kevin was four he knew better than to act like that." For someone trying to keep his other life separate, he sure has a way of rubbing it in Mom's face whenever he's lecturing her about how to be a mom.

Sometimes when Ted is trying to flirt with Mom, he teases her like the boys in my class tease girls, like the other week when I heard them in the kitchen and he said, "Maybe you should ask that crazy old neighbor of yours on a date."

"Leave Mr. Wilkin alone. He's off his rocker when it comes to those animals, sure, but he's never done anything to you. He's lonely since his wife left him."

Of course I knew about Mr. Wilkin; everybody in the neighborhood knew about him. He was the old man with the animals. Some of the older boys in the neighborhood nicknamed him the Zookeeper. It was weird for somebody in Whitney to keep wild animals on their land. I mean *weird*. He was the kind of person that people whispered about, like what he did was so strange that adults couldn't talk about it at full volume.

"That's what I'm saying. If you're so worried about him being lonely, take him out."

"Stop it, Ted. I said I feel sorry for him, but you know I don't like what that man does. He's hoarding those animals like he does everything else," she said.

A few years back, some of the neighbors started asking questions to the local police. That's when we learned it doesn't break any state laws to keep exotic animals on your land. Mr. Wilkin built a makeshift reserve for them: there was a big fence around his whole property and a bunch of smaller fenced-in areas and cages. He didn't take good care of them, though, so the animals' homes started to look like the rest of the things on his land: dingy and worn out. He had at least a dozen beat-up old cars scattered on and around his driveway and even a small plane parked by everything else. I felt bad that he treated the animals the same way as a bunch of junk.

Ted only comes over on weeknights. Most of those times he just follows Mom into her bedroom and she tells me to be good and watch TV with Randy for a while. Ted owns a roofing business; that's how he made all his money. He's not super rich, but enough that he could buy Mom presents sometimes, like a bracelet and a new TV when our old one died. He never tried to buy anything for Randy and me.

Sometimes Ted eats dinner with us, but that's the worst. He doesn't want to talk to Randy and me, that's obvious, but Mom still tries to find something we can all talk about. I don't know anything about roofs, and I don't know what he knows about other than that.

Last night, Ted spanked Randy at dinner when Randy threw his plate of spaghetti on the floor.

"These two need to learn how to behave at the dinner table. And everywhere else."

"They're only children," Mom said. I think she wishes we could stay little forever, maybe so we'd remind her of the time back when my dad or Randy's were around or maybe because she's just scared of us growing up.

After dinner, Mom and Ted got in another big fight. I was in my bedroom when they started yelling in Mom's room and Mom said that she couldn't keep this up. When I walked into the hallway to see what was happening, Ted glared at me and stepped into the hall. He grabbed me by the arm and pushed me back into my room before slamming my door. He knocked me back so hard that I fell onto my bedroom floor. I didn't stand up for a long time.

Ted was gone when I woke up this morning. It was just a regular Saturday with me and Mom and Randy. Mom never works weekends, so we always have that time together.

Sometimes I think Mom is stupid or something because she always points out really obvious things like, "It sure is a cold winter this year." The worst is when she talks about time. She's always talking about how time goes by fast or else acting all surprised when it's daylight savings time again like, "It's staying lighter out longer. Didn't we just change the clocks?" I don't know what it is about older people always being so worried about time. There's a lot of it, and anyway talking about it so much isn't going to slow it down.

Mom did it again today: "It's going to be a hot day. The sun's barely hit mid-sky and it's already sweltering." I've spent my whole life in Nevada; I *know* the summers are hot. Mom was standing in the doorway fanning herself by swinging the screen door back and forth while Randy played with his blocks and I watched TV. One of those reality shows was on where a man falls in love with a bunch of women at once but then he marries the one he loves the most—Mom said shows like that turn my brain to mush, but I like the dresses the women get to wear when they're waiting to find out if the man loves them the most.

On days when Ted didn't come around the house she acted like this, either standing in doorways talking to nobody in particular or else running around the house picking up socks and scrubbing counters. I guess today was too hot for cleaning. She stared out the front door at our yard.

I got my period this morning. I went into the bathroom to pee just like any other time. When I was sitting on the toilet and I looked down at my underwear, I noticed the brown splotch. I didn't know what it was and it kind of freaked me out. I told Mom about it and she got all flustered at first, but then she sat me down on her bed and closed the door and told me what it was. Then she gave me a pad from her bathroom, but I complained because the thing was so huge it looked like a diaper. She told me to use it for now and then we could go to the store later and buy me some tampons.

She said I'd have to stick the tampons up in me. I didn't like the sound of that. I didn't want something inside of me like that. Would I be able to feel it all the time? I asked her. She said I'd get used to it. Or I could stick with the pads. She said I'd have to choose one or the other.

"This is something you'll have to deal with," she said. I didn't understand why I'd have to decide already. I thought this happened to older women with breasts and jobs. Mom cried and said, "Lo, you're a woman now," but I didn't understand how a stain in my underwear could possibly make me a woman.

I wanted to talk to Mom longer and ask her how old she was when she first got hers, but she was in one of those aggravated moods of hers that she settled into when she knew Ted was with his wife, probably worse since they fought the night before. I knew she wouldn't tell me that was the truth, but she always acted like this on the weekends when Ted was with his family.

Ted calls his business "Dr. Roof." He has commercials that play on TV. I always change the channel when they come on. I think one even played right before Mr. Wilkin shot himself; I remember because I was watching cartoons on a local station when the channel was interrupted by the news. We found out about it that way first.

"Hey Mom, you gotta see this," I yelled when "BREAKING NEWS" flashed across the TV screen.

"What is it?" Mom asked, sort of drowsily, letting the screen door glide slowly shut.

"Isn't that our neighborhood?" I pointed to the TV so she would look.

Across the screen, an overhead shot panned across our neighborhood. I could recognize the high school down the street and even the Jamesons' house with the trampoline a block over.

"Yes. What are they saying? Turn it up."

The volume on the reporter's voice rose as she said, "The body of Jonathan Wilkin has been discovered on his land. It appears as though the animals' cages were opened before Mr. Wilkin took his own life. As we said before, please be advised that there are wild animals on the loose. The Clark County Police Department asks that you please stay inside. Do not approach the animals."

"A tiger!" Randy yelled as he touched the screen flashing images of the animals.

Whitney is a suburb of Las Vegas, and it's way smaller and not a place people travel from all over the world to see. Our house is in a neighborhood, but there's still a lot of space between houses. People have big yards, some with tire swings, others with blue plastic kiddy pools with neon fish painted on the sides. One or two families have real pools in the ground that everybody slows down to look at when they pass by.

Mr. Wilkin had the most land of any of our neighbors. He kept a mountain lion, five African lions, three wolves, a tiger, two chimpanzees, and of course the bear. It was a grizzly bear, like the kind I had seen at the zoo on a field trip in second grade.

Mr. Wilkin lived in the neighborhood before my parents moved in and before I was born. Mom said he kept to himself—he never invited people to see the animals. She said she rarely saw him leave his property. His house wasn't directly next to ours (the Campbells and Buckleys are in between), but Mom always kept an eye on him when she drove past his place because she's extra protective of Randy and me. She told us that under no circumstances were we to ever go near his place, let alone try and climb over the fence. Sometimes late at night I could hear the wolves howling, but I never felt afraid. They never seemed dangerous, only out of place.

"Maybe we can look for them from your room, Mom," I said and ran for the bedroom. Mom followed me down the hall.

Mom and me stood on either side of her bedroom window. We couldn't see anything. Her room was in the back of the house, opposite the front yard and the road, but it was closer to Mr. Wilkin's. If we had any chance of seeing the animals, we would see them in the back.

"I can't believe that poor man took his own life," Mom said to me, still looking out the window. "You know his wife left him last year because of his drinking problem. They lost a lot of money when he got fired. I'm sure paying for upkeep to house all those animals didn't help. That Janet was a good woman, but it took her a long time to see what kind of man she was living with. It's a shame. At least she got out when she did," Mom rambled like she does when she's on the phone with one of her sisters.

No animals passed by our window. All I could see in the distance were the tall hotels on the strip. I gave up after a few minutes and sat on the edge of the bed—the side that used to be Dad's.

"It looks so quiet out there," Mom said. She turned and looked at me and then asked, "Where's your brother? Go get him and bring him in here."

I walked into the living room but didn't see him. The TV was still on, playing a seemingly endless loop of images of the dead animals. By that time, the tiger, four lions, and two of the wolves had already been shot by the police. The tiger was found roaming the high school parking lot and the wolves were killed while they rummaged through overturned garbage cans three blocks over. The news showed the four lions in a row lining the street where I had ridden my bike the afternoon before. The police didn't have time to wait for the animal rescue team to bring their tranquilizers. It was a hot summer day and most of the neighborhood kids had set up sprinklers to run through or laid Slip 'N Slides across their front yards.

I moved slowly through the room to the screen door. On the other side, Randy stood in our front yard. Past him, on the edge of the lawn, stood the grizzly. At first it was down on all fours sniffing at the weeds growing through the cracks in the sidewalk. When Mrs. Ronson next door stepped out on her front porch and screamed, the bear stood up. It was so big that its shadow crossed the whole yard, all the way up to Randy, who stood still in his racecar pajamas.

"A bear, Sissy," he said as he looked back at me in the doorway, pointing like we were at the zoo.

I turned back and yelled down the hall, "Mom hurry, it's in our yard!"

I didn't know what she was doing, and I didn't know what I was supposed to do, but I thought I had seen on a nature show that you're supposed to stay still if you encounter a bear in the woods. I opened the screen door and whispered to Randy, "Don't move. Don't move until Momma comes."

The bear looked like it was tired and maybe like it was sick. The temperature was easily over a hundred. The bear wasn't looking at us. He stared at Mrs. Ronson's front door and sniffed the air. Mrs. Ronson had gone back inside, but I could see her standing at her front window, screaming into the phone. I saw a few of our neighbors move into their front yards. They stared at me staring at them, but nobody seemed to want to move. We just stood in this minute-long silence that seemed to last forever. Then we heard the far-off sirens getting closer, and I knew the police were on their way.

Mom finally appeared beside me, holding her rifle. She pushed open the screen door and held it up.

"Lo, get back," she said, and she sounded calm.

It only took her one shot, one blast of sound that tore the air open. It happened faster than my eyes could see. It was more like connecting the dots—Mom and the gun, the sound, the bear, its scream, the blood, the fall, and Randy near it, still.

"You killed it!" I screamed. For a moment nobody moved, like they had to be sure it was really dead before they went any closer.

Everyone around was screaming. Mom was chasing after Randy and then he was in her arms, all wrapped up and lifted off the ground. She tried to cradle him like a little baby even though he's too big for that. The police cars appeared at the end of our driveway and I saw our neighbors with their cameras out taking pictures of the bear. I could smell that metallic smell of the bear's blood; it filled the whole air.

I think I was crying, but mostly I could feel puke in my throat. My stomach had started to cramp so I sat on the front step. Mom laid the gun on the ground; it was so big I didn't know how she was able to hold the thing. I'd never seen her do something like that. I didn't know she could. Randy was quiet, even when everybody else was talking and shouting and asking questions. Randy didn't say anything, just sucked on his thumb and stared at the bear, this heavy clump of fur and blood, like some kind of awful rug decorating our front lawn.

Nobody—not Mom or anyone else—seemed to notice all the blood, but it was all I could see, matted in the bear's fur and splattered across the grass like somebody spilled a paint can. And it was all over my brother—in his hair, on his clothes, smeared across his face. When Mom pressed Randy's face against hers, the blood got on her too. She rubbed the spot on Randy's cheek, but that only made it worse, only spread the thick red like syrup down his face like a wound. I knew that the animal rescue people would come and they'd take the bear away. I knew all the animals would disappear from our neighborhood, mostly shot and dead.

But I didn't know if they could ever clean up all the blood. Even if Mom gave Randy a good bath and scrubbed him with soap, how did you wash it all away? There was so much blood on him.

That's when I saw Ted. He must have come to surprise Mom and was walking up the street toward us (he never parked his car in front of the house). Ted never showed up on Saturdays, but I guessed he was there to apologize for their fight from the night before.

Mom didn't see him walking toward us, but I did. I saw him get about as close as two houses away, see the crowd gathered in the street and driveway, including the police and a news crew with those big cameras, and turn and walk away. Ted walked fast back to his car. He hovered for a moment with his keys in his hand. He looked back toward us.

I looked up and saw Mom staring straight at him. I watched her head move slowly from side to side. I followed her eyes to Ted and watched his face scrunch like mine did when Mom caught me up watching TV past bedtime. It didn't seem like the kind of look I was supposed to see, like it should have belonged to only them. He opened his mouth like he had a question.

Mom hitched Randy up higher in her arms and took my hand. She turned and walked us back to the front door. When

Mom closed the front door and shut out the staring people and the sight of the dead bear, I felt safer, like maybe I could cry in her arms and wouldn't feel embarrassed about it. She moved quickly to the kitchen and didn't stop moving until she had soaked a towel in vinegar and started dabbing at the bloodstains on Randy's shirt. I stood behind her and watched her silently scrub. The only sound came from the crowds outside.

Part of me wanted to look out the window at them, even just a peek through a sliver of space between the curtain and window frame. But I didn't. It was better looking at Mom and watching her hand move faster as the bloodstain grew smaller.

LONGER WAYS TO GO

Rick ordered a stack of pancakes, two eggs over easy, and a couple strips of bacon. Beth's Café was his favorite stop on his haul from Marysville down to Eugene. He liked to eat breakfast food for dinner when he had to make his night drives. It helped the coffee go down easier and, in a way, tricked the body into thinking it was the start of the day instead of close to the end. He figured if it took about six hours each way—and he had to unload in the middle—he wouldn't crawl into bed until after the sun had risen on a new day. He hated the night drives, but he was used to them, and for the last thirty years or so, he'd done them at least twice a week. The thing was, he couldn't tell if they had gotten harder or easier.

He remembered Beth's when it was a little less clean and there were fewer kids around, dragging themselves out of a bar or getting kicked out and coming into Beth's for an omelet greasy enough to hold off a hangover. It wasn't really a place for truck drivers like him anymore now that it was hip, but he stopped in just the same. The coffee wasn't great, but neither was change.

Back on the road, he pointed his truck south and moved from Highway 99 to I-5, the freeway that would take him through downtown Seattle with its few skyscrapers and view of the Sound, past south Seattle, an industrial eyesore, and on through all the gray and uninteresting towns and cities, casinos, and outlet stores that stretched across southwest Washington.

There was a loneliness on the road, an isolation to the job. He spent so many hours alone with his thoughts, things he didn't want as a companion for his drives. Even though he was driving past people all the time, looking over his shoulder to catch a quick glimpse of what their cars held—moving boxes and a nervous-looking young couple, a harried family on a road trip with the kid in the back maybe tugging his arm to get Rick to honk his truck horn in that long tradition of the road—he was only ever looking in. And then passing by.

The coffee went through him faster than he expected. He exited in Tukwila and pulled into the nearest gas station. When he stepped back outside, he shivered in the January air and shook the last bit of water off his hands. He walked to the door of his truck.

"Excuse me. Could you spare a cigarette?" a voice called from behind.

He turned around and saw a young girl sitting on the curb. She looked like she could be homeless, but newly so, like those runaways he saw sometimes in downtown Seattle, hiding from someone and twitching from whatever drug they were on. Her blonde hair hadn't taken on that greasy sheen from too many days without a shower, but she had one of those big camping packs and kept looking from side to side like she was itching to get a move on. She stood and walked toward him.

"You waiting for someone, miss?" he asked as he pulled out a pack of Marlboros.

"I was waiting for someone to give me a cigarette." She winked and pulled one out of the pack. "After this, I'm waiting for someone to give me a ride."

He leaned down and lit the cigarette pressed lightly between her lips before asking, "Waiting for someone in particular?" He couldn't help but stare at her right eye, covered in makeup that wasn't doing its job very well, splotches of purple breaking through to the surface.

"Anyone headed south. I'm going to California."

"By yourself?"

"By myself. I have friends waiting for me down there. I just need to get to them. Are you headed south?" She moved her body a step closer to him like she thought that would help her chances.

He looked at her closely. She barely came up to his chest— probably no more than twenty-one, if that. She could easily have been his daughter. Now he felt bad for the kid.

"I'm headed as far down as Eugene. I can take you there with me. But I want you to understand that I don't usually give rides. If you're running from something or try to pull anything, I'll pull over and kick you right out of my truck. I don't care where we are."

"I'm just trying to get to California," she said and threw her cigarette in the nearby trash.

"Well, get in. We're wasting time standing here."

She ran back to the curb to pick up her backpack and then ran around to the passenger's side of the cab. When she slammed the door, he immediately regretted his decision.

She turned to him with a friendly smile. "What's your name?"

He started the engine. "Name's Rick."

"Pleased to meet you, Rick. My name is Sally Paradise." She reached out her hand and shook his.

He didn't say anything. They got back on the freeway.

"How long you been driving trucks, Rick?"

"'Bout thirty-five years."

"How old were you when you started?" She squirmed a lot in her seat, pulled out her phone and typed on it.

"'Bout twenty-five."

"What brought you to this line of work?"

"Family business. Dad drove trucks, uncle drove trucks."

"Do you like it?"

"Mostly."

"You're not much of a talker, are you Rick? I thought a man like you'd just love to talk. It must get lonely out here."

She pulled out a tub of Carmex, unscrewed the cap as she talked, and rubbed the gooey substance around her lips. He looked at her out of the corner of his eye. She was too skinny. It could be drugs, or just that trend those young girls followed now, starving themselves until they looked like walking corpses. Why they thought that was attractive was beyond him. He remembered growing up and seeing women in the movies who had a little meat on their bones, a waist you could grab hold of. Maybe not all of them. That little Audrey Hepburn had the figure of a teenage boy. Faye Dunaway though, she was good-looking— slim, but with that blonde hair in *Bonnie and Clyde*—and she knew how to hold a gun.

"Do you read much, Rick?"

"Don't have time for it."

"Ever think of investing in books on tape?"

"It would put me to sleep. It's hard enough staying awake on these twelve-hour drives." He looked out the window as they passed Wild Waves Theme Park. It was closed this time of year.

Covered in snow and empty, it always made him shudder when he drove past it. He hated seeing things meant for summer in the wintertime.

"What do you listen to?"

"Baseball mostly. Sometimes country music."

"Oh god."

"What?"

"Like that real southern-fried, God-bless-America twangy stuff?"

"Whatever's on the radio, mostly. I have a couple Merle Haggard CDs and maybe a Johnny Cash in the glove compartment."

"You still have a CD player? What a relic." She opened the glove compartment. Inside was an owner's manual, a few CDs, and a small, half-empty bottle of Jack Daniel's. She held up the bottle. "I can't imagine this helps you stay awake on these long drives."

"It helps me get through them. Now put it away and shut that. Didn't your mother ever teach you not to riffle through somebody's personal belongings?"

"My mother encouraged curiosity. Said it was the byproduct of a healthy, active mind."

"Sounds like a smart type."

"Mother's a lot of things. Cold, mostly."

"Is that why you're running away?"

"I'm not running away. My boyfriend Dean and I are traveling cross-country. See, we started out in New York and meant to go to California. Unfortunately, the last people we hitched a ride with brought us here. By the time we landed in Washington, Dean was so mad at me he told me to find my own way to California. So here I am."

He switched lanes.

"It's not like we won't meet up again in California. Dean just has this temper. He's mad—'mad to live, mad to talk, mad to be saved, desirous of everything at the same time, the ones who never yawn or say a commonplace thing, but burn, burn, burn like fabulous yellow roman candles exploding like spiders across the stars,'" she said and waved her arms around like she was giving a performance in a play. "Do you know what I mean, Rick?"

"Not in the slightest," he answered and chuckled. Girls always loved boys with big dreams.

She sighed. "He's a poet, and he's real passionate—well, mostly he's just crazy, but like I said, he has this temper on him and, well, it's rough sometimes."

"I can tell," he said and looked at her eye.

She waited a moment before she spoke, waited until he had stopped looking at her. "You look like the kind of man who had a daughter that didn't turn out so great. 'Fraid I'll end up like her?"

"I never had a daughter."

"Oh." She slouched in her seat.

After a long silence, somewhere outside of Tacoma, he spoke. "I have a son."

"What happened to him?"

"He went to jail."

She straightened up. "What for?"

"He had a wife, and he did to her what it looks like that boyfriend of yours did to you. He hit her one too many times. She took the kid and left him. Then he went and broke his probation and got hauled off."

"He didn't mean to do it. My boyfriend, I mean. It was an accident."

"The only time I use my fist is on purpose."

He caught her looking at his cracked knuckles, his grip loose on the steering wheel. Too many long hours.

"What about guns, Rick? Are you a gun-toting citizen of this fine country?" She turned her body toward him as she waited for his answer. He could tell she wanted to change the subject. She didn't want to talk about that poet boyfriend anymore.

"Yeah, I keep one."

"Where is it?"

"You ask a lot of questions." He paused, but she didn't respond. "It's in the sleeper. And no, you can't see it."

"Fine by me." Sally moved her attention back to her phone.

He returned his eyes to the road. This girl was distracting. He was almost to Olympia, and he didn't want to miss seeing the capitol building. He had developed superstitions throughout his many years on the road. He considered it good luck to look at the state capitol building on his drives. Then again, he also considered it bad luck to pick up hitchhikers. He had never told anyone about his superstitions. They were silly, he knew, but he still winked at the capitol building as they passed it.

It had been a while since he had done this much talking, especially with a woman, even if she was just a girl. If Donna could see him now. She always used to say he never let anybody near him. Now he was stuck in a tight space with a kid who wouldn't shut up.

"After California, we're thinking about crossing back to New York. Or who knows, maybe even heading down south to Mexico. It's going to be wild. We may as well try it all while we're young. Although we'll probably have to stay in California for a while to work and make some money. It would be easier if Dean had a car. At least it's more interesting this way. Can we pull over soon? I need to use the little girl's room."

"We've barely passed Olympia. Didn't you go where I picked you up?"

"I was sitting out there for at least an hour. You're the first person who looked at me. When you said you'd take me, I didn't have time to stop and think about using the bathroom."

"Can you wait a little longer? I need to make up some time if I'm going to deliver this shipment on schedule." He adjusted his rearview mirror. A small sedan had been driving close behind him for the last half mile, and the glare of its headlights made his eyes ache. "Wait until we get closer to Vancouver."

"I'll try. What do you need to deliver anyway?"

"I'm delivering a shipment of lumber to a hardware store."

"Do you always make the same deliveries?"

"No. I deliver different shipments to different stores around Washington and Oregon."

"Do you own this truck?" He couldn't tell if she was interested or not. She kept putting Carmex on and rubbing her lips at him.

"No. I work for a company that owns semis. They bring in the business and lease the trucks, and I do the driving." He remembered laughing with Donna when they were first married about being called an "independent contractor." It sounded so sophisticated then. They laughed about little things like that.

"When you're not on the road, Rick, where are you?" Could she tell his mind wasn't in the truck anymore?

"I live up in Everett."

"Up north, huh? The couple that dropped me off at the gas station in Tukwila was from Lynnwood. That's up north too, right?"

"I thought the last people dropped you and your boyfriend off together."

She pulled down the visor and looked at herself in the mirror. She ran her fingers through her hair as she talked. "No. Once we woke up and realized we were in Washington, he got out in

Spokane. I tried to tell him that it would be easier for us to take I-5, but he wouldn't listen. I suppose I should have gone with him." She frowned at her reflection and put the visor back up.

"Where are you from, Sally?"

"That doesn't matter. I've come to the West to find freedom and truth, and I don't have a home other than the road now. When you're all done with your delivery and you head back up to Everett, will anybody be waiting for you?"

"No, not anymore."

"Somebody did once, I guess. You have the son."

"Got an ex-wife too."

"What happened? Did she leave you?"

"Yeah. I wasn't around enough. She raised our boy on her own."

"Do you wish you had her back?"

"I wish for a lot of things."

"That's why you've got to figure out how to live your life without any regrets. See, me and Dean, we're so free out here."

He laughed a little to himself. This kid thought she knew what freedom felt like. All she knew was the thrill of a bad relationship.

She must have heard him laugh because she got quiet and looked out the window.

He didn't want to hurt her feelings. She was sweet, and he figured she meant well. He could be so bad at understanding women sometimes. Donna used to say he never took the time to listen to her. He'd never had the experience of a daughter. Letting her sit on his lap and steer his truck. Walking her down the aisle.

"Look, we're near Centralia. We can pull off here. I'll find you a gas station."

Sally wasn't talking anymore, just punching away on her phone. They drove for about a quarter mile off the freeway. On the way to the gas station, they passed a sign for an elementary school.

She turned to him with wide eyes and a grin. "Ooh, let's stop at that school on our way back through. I love schools. They're always the same in a way, even if they look different in each town. And you can always count on them to have a playground, and you know every playground will have a swing set. It must be a regulation."

"I don't have time for that, Sally. I'll barely make it on time as it is."

"Please? It's tradition."

"What tradition?"

"Mine and Dean's. No matter where we are, in whatever small town, we always stop at the public schools and go to their playgrounds. Have you ever looked up at the stars from a merry-go-round? Most schools don't even have them anymore. I guess they're hazards."

They parked at a Chevron. "Go use the bathroom, Sally. And no more stops until Eugene."

"Come on. Haven't you ever had a tradition, something really silly that you do because it makes you feel good?" He looked at her pleading eyes, those eyes that all women possessed—he couldn't explain it, but they had power behind them.

Donna always used to cook him pancakes before his overnight hauls. No matter what, she always did it out of tradition.

"Alright, but no more than ten minutes," he told Sally. "And then no talking for a while." He waited until he was sure she was inside and opened the glove compartment. He just needed one sip if he was going to make it to Eugene.

Sally came back to the truck with a stick of beef jerky. "Here," she said and handed it to him. She mimed like she was locking her mouth shut and throwing away the key. They drove in silence to the elementary school on the way back to the freeway.

"Where's the playground?" he asked as he pulled into the darkened parking lot.

"It looks like this road goes around the back of the school. Follow it."

Around the back, the parking lot showed in scattered lamplight. Beyond the pavement he could see fields of mostly brown grass and a playground stretched over dusty gravel. He could see the worn slide and the dangling swings, but he couldn't find the merry-go-round. Sally'd be disappointed.

"See that car?" he said and pointed. "It looks familiar. What's it doing empty out here?"

"You think I'm the only person who ever thinks to come to a playground when it's dark? There's probably some couple screwing on the baseball field. Don't worry about it. Just park."

"It's January," he muttered to himself.

He checked his rearview mirror once more and parked a few spaces away from the small sedan. He turned off the ignition. She jumped out without a word. He stepped down slowly, watched his breath appear in the cold air. He had his back turned and his hand on the door handle when he heard the safety of a gun click.

"Stay right where you are," a man's voice said from behind.

"Can I turn around?"

"What? Uh, yeah, sure. But put your hands up, and don't move anywhere."

He expected more when he turned around, but instead he got a skinny kid with peach fuzz on his chin wearing a Huskies sweatshirt. He took one hand off the gun to wipe his forehead. The other hand was shaking.

"Now you need to give me your wallet and anything else valuable you have in your truck."

"It's a truck full of lumber, kid. What do you think I've got in there?"

The boy switched hands. The gun wobbled. What was the likelihood that this kid had ever fired a gun before? Rick looked at the little beads of sweat forming on his hairline and bet it was pretty slim.

He slapped the gun out of the boy's hand and punched him hard enough to knock him to the ground. The kid tried to stand back up and got in one swipe to his mouth, but Rick knocked him down before he could stand straight.

"You dumb shit. What do you think this is, a stick up?" he said from above the kid. He looked at his bloodied knuckle and kicked him. It had been a long time since he felt the fleshy, weak part of a stomach give way to his boot. In fact, the last time he'd been in a fight, he'd been on the receiving end. That time outside a bar, right after Donna left. His stomach had hugged the hard tip of a leather boot, then the heel. It felt good to be on the other side again.

He could hear Sally behind him, making a sound somewhere between a cry and a gasp. He'd never had to protect anyone. Rick was not a protector.

"It was her idea," the boy said from the ground. He lay on his side, cupping his stomach.

Rick knelt down and picked up the handgun. It wasn't loaded.

Sally came around the front of the truck. "Please stop," she begged.

He tucked the gun into the back of his pants. "Let me guess. You're the boyfriend. Dean, right?"

"No, it's Craig." He coughed from the ground. "She made up the names, said it would be better that way. *On the Road.* She read it in English last semester. I've never even read the damn book."

"And you're the one who's been following us since I picked Sally up. You little piece of shit. You tried to rob me? I'm a truck driver, dammit. You couldn't have picked someone a little better?"

"You were the first person who offered. We just needed some money," Sally, or whoever, said from behind.

"All this bullshit about being free. You're just a couple of bored kids."

She didn't speak. The kid didn't speak.

"Get in the truck, Sally," he said without looking at her.

She looked at her boyfriend on the ground, then looked back at Rick. "I'd really rather not."

"Don't make me repeat myself." This time he did look at her. Her hands had tightened to little fists. He grabbed her by the forearm and pulled her with him toward the truck, leaving Craig where he lay.

Inside the cab, she reached for the radio controls and turned it to a country station. He turned it back off. He shifted gears and watched the kid in his side mirror as he drove off.

"Pull out your wallet." He kept his left hand on the steering wheel and held out his right hand.

"Are you going to rob me now? Don't you think if I had the money, I wouldn't need to take it from you?" She pulled it out of her purse.

"Open it and hand me your driver's license." Looking like she was about to protest, she glanced at his unflinching face and didn't speak. She handed it over.

"Ashley Baumgartner," he read out loud. "Born in 1996. You're just a kid, Ashley. What are you doing with a guy like that?"

She looked out the window and back at him. "Just having a little fun. You should take care of your lip. It's bleeding on your shirt." She didn't look worried anymore, not now that he'd calmed down and Craig was in the distance. With the gun out of sight, she didn't take him seriously anymore either.

He licked some of the blood away and read her address out loud. "Bellevue, Washington. *Bellevue?* And you had to rob me?"

"Maybe I needed to get away from there. Maybe *he* was the only way out. Maybe we needed a few bucks to get by. That's all."

"I picked you up not more than twenty minutes away from Bellevue. You could have gone home."

"Don't you think if I wanted to be there, I wouldn't have asked you for a ride?"

"I don't think you know what you want, *Sally.*"

She shifted in her seat and faced Rick. "Craig's harmless," she said. As if to demonstrate, she rubbed at her eye until the bruise smeared. "It's only makeup. I thought it would add to the story."

He exited in Kelso and pulled into a gas station.

"What are you doing?" She looked worried again.

"Dropping you off." He pulled out his wallet and gave her a twenty-dollar bill. That was all he had on him. "Call your parents, Ashley. Go home."

"I'll get out here, but that doesn't mean I'm going home. Nobody can make me do it if I don't want to. 'The road is life.'"

"Yeah, whatever that means. It's your life, kid. It's just, I think that . . ." He stopped, took his hands off the steering wheel, and then rubbed them across the seat. "Was the playground part even true? Do you really like to stop at those, or was that part of the setup?"

Those eyes, those big lying eyes. She smiled. "We had to get you somewhere out of the way." She put her hand on the door handle, started to open it, and then turned back. She scooted closer to him. "Thanks for not calling the police or anything."

He started to speak, but didn't.

She put her hands on his face, his skin dry and cracked from the sun. That face that hadn't had hands on it in longer than he could remember. She kissed him once very quickly on the cheek, scooted back to the door, and climbed down.

Rick knew he'd never see her again. He hoped she'd go back home. But he figured she'd probably go back to that kid and that maybe they'd try that stupid plan all over again until someone got hurt worse. Rick pulled back onto I-5 headed toward Oregon. He didn't want to think of the things that crept into his head on these drives: how long until he'd make it to Eugene, and how much longer until he'd make it home.

HUCKLEBERRY SEASON

You sit there, picking at your arm while you drive, like you don't know I'm watching. The skin has browned. When you peel strips off, it looks like the skin on the roasted chicken they served at our reception. That's all I can think about now as the flakes float to the floor: you shoveling forkfuls of chicken into your mouth while I had to do all the talking to *your* relatives.

The cars on the drive up here whip around the blind turns like they have nothing to lose. Where are they all headed in such a hurry? There's nothing out here.

"This is it," you say when you park the truck. "Goddamn, the Cascades are beautiful this time of year."

"We go up to the Cascades all the time to ski at Snoqualmie," I remind you. It looks to me like a bunch of trees, verdant and abundant, sure, but the same kind of trees we passed when we left Seattle to drive to your parents' place in Naches.

"But that's a ski resort forty-five minutes outside Seattle. Chinook Pass is different, quieter. There's not another person in sight." You freeze like you're listening for something. The silence, I guess.

I want to disagree, but you're right. There's a vastness up here that's so great it feels like the whole sky is visible. You open the door and hop down onto the ground, kicking up a cloud of dirt. Your feet disappear momentarily in the storm. I wait for you to come around and open my door, and when you do, I lay my hand in yours and let you pull me to the ground.

"It's been too long since I've been back here. My dad taught me to trout fish up at Rimrock. We could stand around for hours not talking, just waiting for the fish to bite. I'll never forget those summers."

God, David, you always talk about fishing as though it were this secret initiation into manhood that I'll never understand. You're right—I won't understand. Not the fishing or riding four-wheelers or that event you did as a kid in the local rodeos where you rode on sheep—it's like someone plucked you out of a country song and dropped you into my life. There were so many uncertainties I chucked onto the "iffy" pile when we first met that I tried not to think about again. I guess it's funny sometimes how these things turn out: people just come together, like magnets.

"Yes, it is beautiful. And so quiet. I don't think I've ever heard a quiet like this before. You don't get this kind of quiet in Seattle. When I lived in the U-District during college, I don't think I ever heard silence. I had to keep my window open during the summer because of the heat, and I didn't have air conditioning, but then I couldn't sleep because of all the noise. There was always some party going on, or some drunk freshman yelling across the street."

"Yeah, quiet," you say, and you're back to looking at your arm. It's like you think it's the most fascinating thing on earth. I could stand here naked holding a fifty-pound striped bass, and you'd still sit there picking away at your scab like it's your job.

"I'm sorry about your arm, David," I say and reach out to touch you.

But you flinch. "It's still sore," you say. You drop your arms to your side and walk around the truck.

You looked so surprised when I threw that curling iron at you. It surprised me too, I guess. Not that I was so mad at you, but that it could fly like that—out of my hand, the cord yanking from the outlet. It surprised me too how bad the burn was on your arm—still is. I can't tell you that, though, since it was my fault. I can't tell you that it sickened me to watch you pop the blisters over the sink and squeeze until the clear, viscous fluid drained from your arm. Last night, when we had sex in your childhood bedroom, your browned, scratchy skin rubbed across my stomach and I couldn't come. I had to fake it so you wouldn't feel bad.

"Here," you say and push an empty plastic bucket toward me. "We'll each use our own."

"That seems a bit optimistic. Didn't your dad say last night that we're probably a bit late, that the best time for picking is Labor Day weekend?"

"We're only a week off. Besides, I thought it would be easier if we didn't have to share. That way we can split up if we need to."

I have to get away from you, Janey. Sometimes you don't know when to shut your goddamn mouth. My skin is itching like crazy, and all you could talk about on the ride up Chinook Pass was how hot you were. It's summer, for Christ's sake—what do you expect? I'm sorry the air conditioning in the truck is broken, but you bringing it up every five minutes won't make it work again.

When I pulled off the main road and bumped along the dirt road up the mountain, you kept saying, "Slow down" and "Watch out," like I was driving with my eyes closed. I could see the drop-off on your side of the truck too.

My dad used to joke with me after having a few too many beers that a woman is always sweet to you up until you marry her. Then, once she knows she has you, the nag switch turns on. I think you've always had your switch on, but since our wedding, you turned it to full volume.

"Are you in that much of a hurry to get away from me? I thought the honeymoon period wasn't supposed to run out for at least a year. We're eleven months short. You have heard of the honeymoon period, right?" you say to me, and I'd be an idiot if I didn't know that was a reminder that we didn't go on a honeymoon.

You always put me down in the form of a question, like you're not really calling me a loser, just suggesting that I consider the possibility. I wish, Janey, that I had the money to pay for a honeymoon. Hell, I wish I had a rich dad to send me to a private liberal arts college that fed me right from graduation into a design firm that makes bullshit woodland animal logos and chalkboard signs for coffee shops—and somehow still has enough money to provide dental *and* vision insurance plans—but I had to pay for my school, even if all I got was a worthless business degree. I'm still paying. And I wasn't about to let your dad pay for the honeymoon after he footed the bill for that over-the-top reception you thought you needed. I hate taking that man's charity.

"No, baby, it's not like that. The huckleberries are small, and it takes some expert maneuvering to pick them, so it's just easier to carry our own buckets around. Besides, some of the berries are way up there in the steeper parts. I'll have to go up there to pick those myself since you didn't wear tennis shoes."

You look down at your sandaled feet like I insulted you. "I forgot. I'm sorry."

"It's fine. I just wish you would've taken Mom's shoes. That would have made things easier."

"I don't want to wear someone else's shoes, especially not someone's dirty old tennis shoes."

"It wasn't *someone*. It was Mom. It wouldn't have killed you to take them. She was being helpful." You never have taken to Mom. That's fine, since you're such different women. But it isn't fair that you don't even try.

You start to pout. I can see your bottom lip shaking. For such a smart and successful woman, you know how to change into Hurt Little Girl mode fast. All I wanted was for us to spend some time together away from the city. We haven't stopped fighting since we left Seattle.

"Stop, baby—it's okay. Don't get upset. You didn't have to wear Mom's shoes. Your feet will get dirty, but that's okay too. Come on, let me show you what a huckleberry bush looks like."

I kiss you on the forehead because that's how I like to be sweet to you. I like to smell your hair when I do it because it always smells like your lavender shampoo—and that smell always takes me back to our trip to San Juan Island, how you could smell the lavender fields from a mile away and we screwed all over the antique furniture in the bedroom of that bed and breakfast. Today the smell mixes with sweat. You look up, then kiss me. When you bite my lip, I feel better.

You're different from the girls I dated back home, the ones with lower back tattoos who wanted to be dental assistants and nail techs—you've got that ambition about you like you always want more from life and me. You're wearing those short-shorts you think you're too old for, but your legs look great. Long and lean, with a scattering of mosquito bites that mark the days we've been in Central Washington. I tried to trace the roadmap of bites up your thighs last night, but you pushed my hand away and said the heat was getting to you. You're used to mild Seattle weather, nothing like the dry heat here that's so thick you can barely walk through it. Must not have been too hot last night, since I still made you come. Had you howling like a banshee, and I had to cover your mouth so my parents wouldn't hear.

We walk away from the truck and into the first patch of bushes I can find. Leaning over to grab a huckleberry from its bush, I lift it up and show it to you. "See, smaller than a blueberry and darker. These are the plants you're going to find them on. Look for a bit of red in the leaves. Got it?"

"Got it," you say and salute. Sometimes I could just smack you, you're so goddamn condescending.

Huckleberry picking seems like a lot of work for a small payoff. I won't complain, though, because that's exactly what you expect me to do. You were offended when I wouldn't camp with you, hurt when I said I thought fishing for sport was cruel. If coming up to the mountains and plucking tiny berries all afternoon will make you feel better, I can make that sacrifice.

I feel uneasy up here among the sharp cliffs and roughly cut edges. There's something claustrophobic about this silence blanketing everything. There's nobody else up here but you, and this emptiness makes me feel like we're trapped together on a desert island.

I find a small patch of berries near you and start picking. Mostly I'm watching you. I like the scrunched look on your face as you concentrate, even if you keep scratching at your arm. You move with animal quickness between grabbing a huckleberry and clawing at your skin. I always thought your athleticism was sexy, like when you worked as a bike messenger after college and used to come back to the apartment sweaty from biking hills all day. But I worry that with the scratching, you'll make the scarring even worse. I want to tell you to stop. It's your wound to pick, though, so I move back to the huckleberry bush.

"Oh God," I blurt out when the biggest ant I've ever seen walks across my toes. I kick my feet and stumble backwards.

You turn and grab my arm. "Be careful out here, baby. I don't want my new bride to tumble down the mountain."

"Thanks. You wouldn't believe the size of that bug. It was like a mutant."

"That's nature for you."

That's nature for you. God, that's such a stupid thing to say. A year ago, when a blank look went over your face when I'd mention a favorite author of mine, or those first few months after you got the new job and you would drone on about your day at the office even though I was painfully bored listening to stories about selling copiers, I couldn't figure out why we were still dating. But we're here now, and I think that's what matters. I think we've made it over the hump. At some point a person has to accept that adulthood looks different from how you imagined it as a child. At some point, you cut your losses and settle with what you have.

There are things I love about you. There are *plenty* of things. You stand up for me. And you're probably heroic. When we first met at that party and you danced goofily with all that cocky entitlement because you're a good-looking guy, I knew you would be pretty but a little dumb for it. You're kind, most of the time. And you use your hands—you helped build that deck at your parents' house your dad showed off yesterday, and you work on your truck. When you look at me, I feel loved earnestly. I can't forget those things. It's easy to forget those things.

But I can't have this kid with you. Your good qualities don't make you ready to be a dad; they make you a sensible choice for a husband who needs to grow up a lot before we can even think about raising a child.

I won't have this kid with you, even if you don't know there's a kid to be thinking about. As I watch you digging on your knees through the huckleberry bush like some kind of foraging animal, you look so sweet and unassuming. I'm scared you'll tell me to cancel my appointment next week. You'll say nobody is ready to be a parent, but that doesn't solve the problem of us being unprepared—it simply means we're in poor company. I'll take care of it myself, and you'll be spared the internal debate and the guilt over what we both know is the right choice. You're too idealistic, so I had to make this decision for the both of us.

I can feel you right behind me, just standing there. Your boredom feels like a heavy load on my shoulders. You probably picked only one huckleberry before you started yawning and staring at your nails. Now you keep leaning over my shoulder going, "There's one" and "Did you see that one? Don't miss it." You might as well climb on my back, and I'll carry you around with me.

"I'm going to hike up there," I say and point to the steepest incline I can find, enough of a hike that I know your sandals and your distrust of nature will keep you from following me.

"Why do you have to climb so far up?" you ask, and you look back and forth between me and the mountainside as if you're deciding whether to fight me on this.

"It's all picked through down here. The only chance we have of leaving here with a full bucket is if I go up to the harder spots. I just have to hope nobody got there first."

"Okay," you say in a way that drags the word out. You look at your feet and back at me. "Please be careful. And please don't go so far away that I can't see you. And please don't go where I can't hear you either. And call to me in a few minutes so I know you're okay. You won't try anything stupid, right?"

"Calm down, baby. I'll be right up there," I say and point again.

I cross the dirt road and dig my feet into the ground as I start climbing. I've got the bucket pushed up into the crook of my elbow so I can have both hands free to grab onto plants if I lose my footing. I feel like a kid at the beach this way, like maybe I'm about to build sandcastles instead of pick huckleberries. The bucket's on my arm with the burn mark. It doesn't hurt; it didn't really hurt at all when the iron burned me, it happened so fast. But I keep picking at it because it's gross as shit and I can't stop looking at it, and also because every time I pick at it I know you're watching. It feels good for you to be the one who made a mistake for once.

Last week you saw the letter from the bill collector. You were crying in the bathroom when I found you.

"Were you going to tell me about this? Or were you just going to ignore this bill like you ignore any other inconvenience?"

"Calm down, baby. Calm down. You have to wait and let me explain these things to you before you get so upset." I held your head in my arms as you sat and cried on the bathroom counter. "I got a little behind on the utilities payment because I didn't make as much on commissions last month. Sales have been shitty these last couple of months, but they'll pick up," I assured you.

"So tell me. We move some things around, cut back on what we don't need. I know we don't make a lot, but it only makes it worse if we start getting behind." You said "we," but I knew you meant I didn't make a lot. "You can't let these things escalate, David. We're adults; don't you think you should act like one?" Just because it was true didn't mean you had to say it like that.

"I'll get the money. We'll be fine. I can sell the truck if I have to." I didn't want to sell my truck, so I knew I would have to figure something else out—maybe we couldn't split all the bills halfway like I made you promise we'd do when we moved in together. "It's alright. This stuff has a way of working itself out."

"You have to understand that I worry about these things. I have a reason to. We're making a life together. You should have told me so I could step in and pay for it."

"You've got to calm down about this kind of stuff. So we're a little behind. Between the two of us working, we're making it just fine. I can go back to the bar I worked at in college and pick up an extra shift if I have to." I didn't want to go back to that. It was bad enough when I first met your parents and your asshole dad looked at me like I was a loser when I told him what I did; if I had to go back to that job, he'd never take me seriously. He barely does even with my sales job.

"I know; I'm sorry. I'm emotional right now," you said as you rubbed the tears off your face. Your mascara had run, and I knew we would be late for the party we were supposed to go to.

I grabbed the bill and moved to the door of the bathroom. "Are you on your period or something?" I asked, as a joke. You're so serious sometimes.

That's when you threw the curling iron at me and burned my arm to shit. I was so angry with you. Sometimes you can be such a crazy bitch. I wanted to pick it up and throw it back at you. Better yet, hold it down on *your* arm, but it was my fault you were upset, so I didn't.

You slammed the bathroom door, and we didn't talk about the burn again until today. I had to tell my parents that I burnt myself at work. They should have asked me how I could have done that in an office building, but they're smart enough to have caught my look that told them to drop it.

I can still see you from up here. I look up to check on you every couple of minutes to make sure you're okay. I've found one huckleberry bush with enough berries on it to keep me from looking like a jackass for climbing all the way up here. I've got a system going: pick ten berries, check on you, and then check on the bucket. The bucket disappoints me. It seems like it's getting emptier instead of fuller. I keep squishing the huckleberries between my fingers from pulling on them too hard. This is becoming less and less worth it. Huckleberries are too small and bitter anyway.

At least there's the silence up here. I love it in the mountains. The great outdoors. I love to shout into the air knowing that not a single soul will hear me. You don't get that feeling living in the city. Feels like there's always someone around.

Below me you're smaller, and you're crouched over a bush with your ass in the air. It makes me laugh because you look sort of childish, and yet somehow still sexy. When we first met, I stared at your ass. It's round and almost too big for your small frame. I'll never forget the night we met at my friend's party. You were wearing that tight dress, and I was making you laugh with my moves. You were so smart and gorgeous; it intimidated me. I didn't know if I would be good enough for you, but I wanted to try.

You can be so sexy when you don't know anybody's looking, like now, when I watch you from all the way up here. I can still

get a hard-on just staring at you, bent over with your shorts riding up your thighs. I hope that feeling I get when I look at you
lasts a long time. When I see you all made up wearing lipstick at
a party, or even in your underwear and a tank top when it gets
too hot in our apartment, you're the only one I want to be with.
All the other stuff, the fighting and your parents always getting
in our business and the way you talk to me sometimes like I'm a
kid, I know that's just the stuff you have to work at in a marriage.
Someday down the road you'll be a mom, and hopefully you'll
calm down a little and you'll let me be the provider. I could be
good at taking care of you if you'd just let me.

The silence is all-consuming. Everything I step on—broken
branches or scattered rocks—sounds louder in the still air. I keep
looking up to make sure you haven't disappeared. You haven't,
but you look far away up there. I've barely covered the bottom of
the bucket with huckleberries. It seems pointless now.

I sit down on a big rock. I'm starting to sweat, and I wipe my
forehead. The sky is clear right now. I'm almost thankful for the
bees that start buzzing around me because it gives me something
to listen to. When it's quiet, I feel alone. I swat at one and then
jump up and run when it won't leave. I don't want to be left
alone in this silence. It's like the truck ride up here. It's like that
night after we fought, when you kept your sleeves rolled down
and wouldn't talk to me at the party, just kept grabbing beers
and looking the other way.

Don't you know I do these things because I'm trying to help
you? I know you have all this potential. The other guys, they made
more promises than you, made all the big, sweeping gestures,

but they always left. You stayed. You weren't the smartest or the most successful, but that's not everything. You were sweet to me, and you were there, and after you held me in the night, you were still there in the morning. It's not that I think I'm better than you; it's that I'm farther along. I had things figured out sooner. It doesn't mean you won't figure things out too. You'll grow up and learn to take better care of yourself. I'm simply here to get you to that place sooner.

You've got this thing in you—I see it when I look into your eyes and don't look away. There's something good in there, like you'll love me forever. You've got to grow up and settle down, David. I can't have a baby with you until I can stop taking care of you.

When I look back up at the spot where you were standing, I don't see you anymore. I take a few steps toward the dirt road to get a better look, but you're still not there. I can't hear you either, not the sounds of your steps, or your breathing, or anything.

"David," I call, and then I hold my breath and listen. No response. "David, are you there?"

I scan my eyes around the area I last saw you, past the dirt road, the prickly weeds and wildflowers, the scattering of huckleberry bushes, and the occasional boulder. I stop briefly on a large shape near the top of the slope, but it's a tree stump, so I move on.

"David, can you hear me?" I yell the loudest I've maybe ever yelled, louder than the yells we use when we fight. This yell is not anger—it's desperation. My mind begins to race. I pull my cell phone out of my pocket, but there isn't a signal up here. You have the keys to the truck. I shouldn't move my thoughts in this direction, but I can't seem to stop them.

I think of *tumbling*, of *falling*, of *descending*—words that bring you down. I think of *cliff* and *abyss*—words with edges. I think of you on the ground, your body crumpled. "David," I call, quieter.

I picture myself walking back down the dirt road, waving down a car, and returning to your parents' house. I see a search party forming, tears and news cameras, flashlights and dogs. I imagine us finding you after a week of searching, my beloved husband, father to a son or a daughter that I'll have to keep considering the circumstances, and if it's a son I'll give him your name. I think of raising our child alone, of how long it will take to get over you. What am I supposed to do being stuck with a daily reminder of you?

I call out your name again when I hear a cascade of small rocks rolling down the hill and see a cloud of dust. I wonder if loneliness is a stronger feeling than love.

"David! David, where are you?"

"I'm right here, baby."

"Oh, thank God."

"It's okay. Are you okay?"

"No. I thought you disappeared."

"Where would I have gone?"

"Anywhere. It's so big and empty up here. I thought I lost you."

"You won't lose me, baby. Come here. I'm always here for you."

"Kiss me, David. I need you to kiss me hard so I don't feel scared anymore."

"Is this how you want me to kiss you?"

"Yes, yes, David."

"What else?"

"I want you right here. I want you on top of me here, like this."

"Out here on the ground?"

"Yes, here. I need to feel you close to me."

"Did you bring the condoms?"

"No, I don't care. I need to feel close to you again, right now. Put yourself inside me."

"Is this good?"

"Yes, like that. Do it like that, slow, yes, like that. I love feeling you inside me, David. I need to feel you here. I love having your arms around me."

"What else do you like?"

"I love it when you hold me. I love it when I can feel your hands on my back. Scratch me like that, David."

"Uh huh."

"Dig your nails into my back. Deeper. Tear me apart."

"Tell me what you want, baby."

"I want you. I want you to never leave me."

AFTER THE WORLD ENDS

The dust will settle over the newly raptured earth. This earth will not look like the earth you knew in the days before. It will be torn apart in too many places to count—ravaged by earthquakes, tornadoes, and hurricanes. It will be split open, like a mother giving birth to new life, but there will be no new life, only death, and finally, destruction.

This is how my mother described the end to me. All I could picture were the five months after the rapture and before the supposed end, when believers would be up in heaven and I could finally enjoy a little peace and quiet at home.

Dust had been collecting in our home. Momma didn't think it mattered much anymore, but it bothered me, thinking about the little particles of dirt and skin floating through the air, covering bookshelves and windowsills, finding their way into us with every breath.

My mother first heard Harold Camping's message one Saturday afternoon as she flipped through the TV channels. We couldn't afford cable anymore, and nothing good ever came on regular television on Saturdays at three. I was passing through the living room on my way to the kitchen and caught a brief glimpse of him—a decrepit old man who looked like death would take him long before his rapture ever did. He sat sunken in a big leather chair in front of an overflowing bookshelf. He had a large Bible opened on his knees that he glanced at occasionally. I watched as the self-taught Bible "scholar" looked out at his audience and said with utmost certainty that he knew when the world would end. I couldn't help but think how self-assured he was, but then I left the room and stopped thinking about him.

"What do you think of this?" Momma had called to me from the couch.

"Think about what?"

"The world ending like he says it will."

"I don't know. I think maybe Mr. Camping's a sad man, and he wants to believe in something."

"I guess. For all we know, he could be right." I didn't know how much she thought about going to heaven; I thought Momma was focused mostly on this life being over with.

At only sixteen, I had just discovered Kurt Cobain, started sneaking cigarettes from my mom's pack, and was still a virgin. The furthest I had gotten was a boy feeling me up after a dance. My parents didn't raise me with religion. They taught me to respect my elders and not to swear in front of strangers. We didn't go to church on Sunday mornings, but we did camp at Moses Lake and eat dinner together, so we were just as good as any other family. Until last year when my dad left, and now it's just Momma and me. He promised it wasn't my fault, just said Momma was so sad all the time and he didn't know how to make her happy anymore. He didn't say where he was going, but I guessed it was far away from Ellensburg. He didn't ask me to come, but if he did, I would have said yes.

After my dad left, all my mother could afford to drink was beer. It was in the last couple of months that she stopped dressing herself. I'd come home from school and find her in one of the old, baggy T-shirts he left behind from softball teams he once played on or concerts they went to long ago. Before I could start my homework or cook us dinner, I would sit down on the couch and brush her hair. She'd move to the floor and I'd sit behind her, silently combing through the tangles. Some days she would want me there more than others. I'd try to leave and she'd say, "Please, baby, just a little longer. Will you please make me look nice tonight?"

She was beautiful still, even in her thirties. I think she just forgot it sometimes because she was lonely.

"Sometimes I wish I had your hair," she would tell me. "Always so perfectly straight. You didn't get stuck with my frizz."

"I love your hair, Momma. You've got curls."

"You're too good to me. You're sweet, and a good liar." This made us laugh. "If I still looked like you, I'd have boys calling the house for me all the time too. Don't get me wrong, I had them in my day. I had a lot of them, mind you."

"I never doubted it. You dated a marine once, didn't you?" I asked, even though I knew the answer.

"Yes, I did. He took me to the Marine Corps Ball and everything. I must have been about eighteen. But nobody was ever as handsome as your daddy, I swear it. Come on, let's switch. It's your turn."

I liked the days when we'd switch places. I liked to feel her fingers in my hair. When I was little, she used to put those tiny sponge curlers in my hair. She'd twist and pull and wrap my hair around until I cried. She always promised it would be worth it in the morning. She'd wait for big events like class pictures, and once she promised to stay up with me until I fell asleep, said she'd even put curlers in her hair too.

I have a memory of Momma and Dad together from back before he left; it was the last family vacation we took. We drove to the Oregon Coast: Cannon Beach first, and then Manzanita. There's a hidden beach between the two towns called Short Sand Beach. You have to park your car and walk on a trail through the woods before it opens up onto the beach. This part of the trip was my favorite, especially when we crossed the wobbly bridge and Dad let me bounce on it, even though it made Momma worry.

We went in the early spring, so it rained—not a heavy winter rain, but a misty drizzle that was so light you barely realized you were wet until you looked down and saw all the beads of water collecting on your coat. It was foggy, and the tide was low, so we could walk really far out and look back and barely see the shore. This scared me, but Momma held my hand and walked with me. We were lucky and timed it right—after lunch but before late afternoon—so nobody else was out on the beach but us. All we could hear were the waves. Momma didn't say much about God back then, but when she got extra quiet and stared out at the ocean, I figured this was why she wore a small cross around her neck.

At the end of the trip, I cried once we crossed back into Washington. Sometimes faith is just a way of giving yourself a nicer-sounding truth.

The day of Harold Camping's rapture, I came home and found my mother sitting on the couch wearing a white sundress. Her skin looked darker against the white cotton. The past month,

Momma stopped paying the utility bills because she said they didn't matter. I had to beg her to write the check so the power wouldn't get turned off. Once, I even forged her handwriting. She started marking the kitchen calendar with X's to show the countdown until the rapture. I had asked her how she knew Harold Camping was right, and she had said, "Baby, some things you've just got to have faith in." That wasn't a good enough answer, but she didn't seem to care.

She stood up and twirled. "It's pretty, huh? I haven't worn this in years," she said as she tugged at the hemline. "Oh, and look, I brushed my hair out and I found my old red lipstick. Do you think it's too much?"

"Are you going to a rapture or a dance?"

"Hush. I want to look my best. Baby, tonight at six o'clock, I'm going to be taken from this earth and up into heaven. Me. Can you believe that? I'm just sorry you don't want to come with me." She said this part like I had misbehaved, like I had forgotten to clean my room or take out the trash.

"I know, Momma," I said as I passed her on my way to the kitchen.

"It's not too late. Maybe if I want it enough, that will get us both in."

Could you take a guest to the rapture? I wondered. "What do you want for your last meal, Momma?"

"It doesn't matter much to me. I can heat up some leftovers. Can you fix me a drink? I'm so thirsty."

"Do you really think you should drink right before the rapture, Momma?"

"I just want one beer to take the edge off. I don't want to be so anxious when I meet my maker. Your grandpa, my daddy, he used to always have a sip of something before we went to church. We'd go to the seven-thirty mass—Catholics like to get up real early. I don't think my mother ever knew about it, but I caught him once slipping a little whiskey into his coffee, and he told me someday he'd let me have a sip."

"Did he ever let you?" I called from the kitchen.

"No, he must've forgotten. 'Course, he died when I was just a girl." Momma lost her dad when she was just thirteen, even earlier than I lost mine. Not that mine couldn't come back.

"His liver, right?" I asked as I handed her a beer.

"Yeah, I suppose it was." She put the bottle to her lips and held it for a moment before she took a slow drink.

We ate our dinner on the couch—warmed-up tuna casserole—in front of the TV. Momma said she needed to pay attention to the news. Soon, she expected special reports to blast across the screen telling us of all the natural disasters that would simultaneously occur throughout the world.

"Oh, Momma, you wouldn't believe what happened in biology yesterday." Our teacher, Mr. Hale, had been lecturing about Darwin and evolution. Then Samantha, this Mormon girl from a real strict family, handed him a note from her dad that said she didn't have to be subjected to teaching that went against "the Word of the Lord." There was a big fuss, and the principal had to come in. We ended up watching a movie from the Discovery Channel about animal survival in the Sahara Desert.

"Hush, baby. Not right now. I have to pay attention." The weatherman on the television reported that tomorrow would be mostly cloudy with a chance of rain.

"Any minute now, any minute now," she chanted as she looked out the front window. She wiped her mouth and dropped her napkin onto her plate. She took another drink of beer, and I could hear her swishing the liquid around like mouthwash. I cleared the TV trays and walked the dishes to the sink.

"Don't worry about those dishes," she called to me. Then to herself she said, "I don't have to worry about nothing now."

At six, she ran to the front door like she was expecting a visitor. She flung it open and stood in the doorway, her arms held out at her side. She must have stood there for a good five minutes with her eyes closed. I watched her from the couch and kept the news on mute. Then her arms dropped back to her sides, her eyes opened, and she slammed the door shut. I held my breath.

"Unmute the TV. Flip through the channels. I gotta see if there's any earthquakes."

An hour passed, and she didn't move from the couch. I washed the dishes, clipped my nails, and waited for her to say something.

After some time, I stretched my arms and looked cautiously at her. "Maybe Mr. Camping was wrong, Momma."

"Do you think I'm not aware of that? The world's still spinning, ain't it?"

"I meant maybe his calculations were just a little off. Maybe he got the wrong day. It could be tomorrow, for all we know."

"Tomorrow could be the rapture?"

"Yes, Momma, it could be."

"But what if it doesn't come tomorrow?"

"Then maybe it will come the day after that. You just sit right here, and you keep waiting."

"I want to light some candles. Bring me the tall white candles we used to put out when your daddy lived here. Remember when I used to make him spaghetti and meatballs and I'd set the table with a tablecloth and use the nice candles? Do we still have those?"

I searched through kitchen drawers, past old bills, a broken can opener, a letter from my father that came with his last child-support check, and half a dozen lighters. I cracked the window and lit a cigarette while I searched.

"Bring me a drink, too," my mother called from the living room. "I think I have some red wine left. You can have a little. We may as well use up the good stuff. This is my wedding night. I'm going to be a bride again, and Lord Jesus'll be my groom. Did you hear that, baby?" She was starting to slur her words, part excitement but part having too much to drink. Those two often went together.

I sat on the counter by the window, blowing long, practiced puffs of smoke through the opening. Only two more years until my eighteenth birthday—then I could leave her. I stubbed out my cigarette and pulled down a glass to pour wine for her. The glass left a circular imprint in the dust on the shelf. I grabbed a second glass, blew the dust off the bottom, and poured it for myself. Then I found two white candles, burnt nearly down to the bottom. I figured they would do.

"Maybe put on some music too."

"My choice?" I asked

"Your choice, baby."

I set everything down on the coffee table and lit the candles. We each held a glass of wine in one hand and a candle in the other, careful not to spill. My mother set her candle in the holder on the table and motioned for me to do the same. She grabbed my hand and squeezed it. I checked the wrinkles on her hand against mine.

"Oh, come Lord Jesus, come," she whispered.

At some point in the middle of the night, I dropped my head onto her lap, and she ran her hands through my hair. I closed my eyes as she twisted long strands around her fingers.

"Never should trust a man who makes big promises. Forever is too big a promise. Can't promise fifteen years—how could I expect eternity?" she whispered to herself before she blew out the candles and sat back, fixing herself into the crack between the couch cushions.

I thought she'd tell me to get up and go to bed, but she didn't. If I could have stopped everything right then, I might have done it, just so it could be the last thing we did. I stayed up with her all night, keeping the vigil.

NO HORSE IN THIS RACE

Dad comes home looking the worst he has in the month since he lost the lawsuit. I'm used to it now, the way the door slaps shut like I imagine the judge's gavel did during the trial even though Dad explained that it was a civil case and not a criminal one, and that the kind of stuff I watch on TV didn't really happen.

When we were kids, my sisters and I used to run to the door to meet my dad after work, begging for candies he brought back from the front desk in his office when Mom had her back turned in the kitchen. After she left, we stopped running to meet him. Instead, my sisters hid in their bedrooms and I made myself small in any nook I could find—the bathtub with its new ring of soap scum or the closet under the stairs where Dad put all Mom's stuff just in case. I read until he found me, which he inevitably did, a game of hide-and-seek he never started but always ended.

I'm not a kid anymore, but sometimes the sound of the door slamming makes me feel like I am, like I did something bad and don't know it yet. My fingers grip the edge of the table as I wait for him to speak.

"They want the horses. They want the goddamn horses," he says and pounds his fist on the table, a gesture that tells me it's really bad, like when he first found out his employees were suing him.

I don't speak—I never speak when he wields his hand like a weapon, fingers splayed. I grab the homework I have spread out and busy myself cleaning up so I can start on dinner. He sits down next to me at the long oak table that has been in this dining room since I was a kid, able to hold twelve people during the holidays. Since my sisters moved out and Grandpa passed, most nights it's only the two of us. This house is large enough for a family of five plus company, but most days there are rooms we never enter, light switches we never flip.

He drops his face into his open palms and mumbles, "How do they expect a man to pay a million-dollar judgment just like that?"

With the horses, I figure. But I won't say that to Dad. *You know what happens to smart mouths.*

"Those bastards start poking around my assets, looking into my personal business. A man can't make an investment? I made it during this whole mess. It's not like I rushed out the door after they read the verdict and stuffed my money into a mattress. They act like I'm some no-good, hillbilly criminal. I *invested* in the horses."

A month ago, I heard him on the phone talking about the threats to garnish the wages he paid my brothers-in-law if he didn't pay up. I didn't know the term and could only picture food at steakhouses. Now there's talk about them coming after our property or the houses my sisters and their husbands own, big places like ours nestled into acres of farmland we don't farm. Mostly the fields are open to all my young nieces and nephews, miles-long stretches of playgrounds just for them.

Sometimes I play tag with them in my sister Rachel's yard or Marco Polo in the little lake near my sister Rebecca's place, but it's hard enough trying not to be seen as a baby when you're the youngest. I don't need to hang around all their babies and make it worse. My sisters don't have much time for me since they started their own families. I don't talk to them much about Dad's temper—it's best to be quiet and wait it out. Someday I'll get to leave like they did, but not to get married and have kids. I don't want the boring lives they have. I want to be free, untethered. But for now, I am bound to this life by Dad.

I was ten when Mom left, sixteen now. For the first year or so, when Rachel and Rebecca were busy playing sports or baby-sitting to get out of the house, Dad would look at me and say, "What am I going to do with you?" I never answered. I wasn't sure what to say, like it was a question for grown-ups. Now when I close my eyes and picture the way Dad looked at me, I think he saw me as one of those changelings in bedtime stories. After two girls, Dad wanted a boy, but instead he got me. I don't know why Mom left, but Dad blames me for it, like my ten-year-old self had whispered into Mom's ear to run. Sometimes, in my dreams, I think I did. Other times I dream she took me with her.

"What are you going to do?" I ask him now.

"What am I going to do?" Dad repeats without looking at me. He stands with a jolt and pushes his chair too hard so that it knocks into the table, sending a shiver through me. He walks to the liquor cabinet and pulls out a bottle of Maker's Mark. He must have six bottles in there, like he's stocking up for the rapture.

I rise and walk silently to the kitchen, the easiest place for me to disappear without question. I hear Dad switch on the television and flip through the channels until he lands on the one where the anchors deliver the day's news by yelling at you. In my rush to make a quick dinner, I burn my arm while cooking the bacon. It continues to crackle while I bite down on my tongue and feel my skin throb with angry heat. There's no time to run it under the faucet. It's like Dad and I are racing each other. I need to get the food on his plate before he pours another drink or else I lose.

We eat our BLTs in silence—him thinking and me waiting. I watch his mouth pinch as he chews and his shoulders slump. I don't think daughters are supposed to see their fathers this way.

"Times like these, I wish my dad was still around. Maybe he'd know what I should do about this mess," he says as he stares at the front door, like he expects Grandpa to come walking through it. Dad never talked fondly about Grandpa when he was alive. He talked about him like he was an unwanted houseguest who had overstayed his welcome before arriving.

"Don't you have to pay it? If they won the case, don't you have to pay them what you owe or else you'll get in more trouble? Couldn't you go to jail?"

"Don't ask questions you don't want the answers to, Ruth-Anne," he says and pushes his empty plate away from him, like it's a thing that disgusts him, a dead raccoon on the highway, his childhood. He stands and makes his way back to the liquor cabinet as I clear the table.

If they arrest him, it will be just me in this big house—and no horses to take care of, since they'll take them too. I've shared a house for sixteen years with my parents, siblings, and grandpa. I've rarely had a moment to myself here. I wonder what it would feel like to move from room to room and hear nothing but my own breathing? I could become a ghost here and haunt this place, like our memories of the times before Mom left.

These racehorses weren't the first we had. When I was six, Rebecca was twelve, and Rachel was fourteen, Mom inherited a retired racehorse from a sick cousin in Auburn. Dad protested, but Mom pointed to our empty acres and used the three of us girls as a chorus of support against my father.

Dad let us take turns feeding and brushing the horse's mane. He had the name Cletus left over from his previous life. We begged for a name change—Buttercup, Daisy, or Swift, anything that didn't sound like somebody's cruel uncle. Dad said it wouldn't be right calling the horse something else after he had the same name his whole life.

"You've got to respect a legacy. Taking away a racehorse's name is like burying a man without a headstone."

Cletus had never won any races. He was sickly when he arrived. Less than a year later, we lost him. He was the first loss I experienced, a bad omen of things to come. He was sick and whinnying with pain. One night I woke to the sound of a gunshot and ran downstairs. I hovered near the front door until Dad came inside.

Dad spoke to me as he took off his coat and boots: "When a creature gets to that point, Ruthie, you have to understand that it needs to be put out of its misery. It's not the easier choice, but it is the right one."

After the war, Grandpa made his living writing obituaries for the *Enumclaw Courier-Herald*. He called his obits section No Horse in This Race. When I was twelve I asked him why, and he said it was 'cause anyone who appeared in his section no longer had a horse in any race.

"People say life is a rat race—you've heard the phrase before, haven't you, Kid?" Grandpa asked me.

"Sure," I said and nodded, even though I hadn't. Grandpa hadn't always called me "Kid." It started around the time my mother left. It was a nickname that kept me at a distance, as though the offspring of his absentee daughter-in-law was likely as unreliable as her mother. I became his favorite by force of necessity. The other girls got boyfriends one-by-one and left home. Since he got along better with me than with his own son, I became his unlikely ally, and since I felt safer around him than Dad, he became mine. The least wanted, the throwaways, will turn to each other so they can feel like someone needs them.

"Well, I'm a horse man myself," he answered matter-of-factly.

Grandpa retired from the paper, though Dad said otherwise whenever he had too many beers in him and felt enough resentfulness toward Grandpa for growing up poor: "Get fired from the job you've had thirty years because you're obsolete—that's what you get working for a section that can be written in twenty minutes by another reporter."

Grandpa never fought him on that. Said he was proud of his hard work. "Writing obits has meant more to me than fighting in any war has. At least this way I'm preserving people's lives, not destroying them."

My sisters married men who were like my father, not necessarily in looks or personality but in hulking presences. When they became managers of Care-All Drywall, Dad took out ads in the *Enumclaw Herald-Courier* about the "family business." He even shot a commercial with us all lined up in front of the office—Mike and Rebecca and their three kids on one side, and Adam and Rachel and their two kids on the other side. Nobody mentioned Mom's obvious absence or Grandpa's being left out.

I stood at the end near Rebecca's youngest like a piece of furniture kept in a separate room because it didn't quite match the rest of the set. Finally, Dad had sons to work for him. *What's a man without a son to carry on his legacy?*

He tried his darnedest to make the most out of having girls, but I overheard him once telling Mom that he lost Rachel and Rebecca to "damned hormones—girls only want to put on make-up and talk on the phone to boys." I wore overalls, kept my shoes muddy. Dad taught me how to use a gun when I was ten and a half. It was after Mom left; she would have never let me near one.

Dad pulled out his shotgun and lined up tin Folgers cans along the fence. He showed me how to load it and remove the safety. He kneeled beside me and put his arms around me to show me how to hold it. It felt like a reverse hug. I curled into his touch and felt the gun's weight when he let go. A mother bird forcing her baby's flight. The gun felt as heavy as the time I made a bet with my sister that I could hold ten rocks of her choosing from the nearby creek and she chose the kind she had to drag and lift with both hands in one swoop to reach my arms.

"Got to learn. It's tradition in the family. Great-grandpa passed it on to Grandpa who passed it on to me. Now I pass it on, to my daughter in this case. Some things are tradition. Grandpa may be a mean son of a gun most the time, but he's a damn good shot."

I missed every can I aimed for, but I only stumbled back the first time, my body unprepared for the force of release. Dad took the gun away from me, reloaded, and shot each can in a row. Dominoes.

"You can forget about hunting."

I looked at my feet and thought I didn't want to hunt anyway. I didn't want to kill anything—I just wanted to show Dad I could if he needed me to.

Dad came home confident the first evening of the trial. I ran up to him, like one of those *Little House on the Prairie* girls waiting for Pa to give them news from the outside world before they had the internet.

"It's gonna be okay, Ruthie. We're going to be fine." He kissed me on the forehead in the way he used to tuck me into my purple pony bedspread. "There's no way these yuppie Seattle *lawyers* are going to come down here and tell me how to run a business. I've been in Enumclaw my whole life. I know what I'm doing."

I didn't think "lawyer" was a bad word, one that Dad needed to lower his voice around me to say.

"Did they look guilty, your employees?"

Up until then, in the sluggish months of depositions and hearings, all the undramatic buildup to a trial, Dad refused to give me details. It didn't concern me. It was about business.

"Come on," Dad said and waved me to follow him outside. "Let's feed the horses."

We walked along the freshly mowed green of our backyard toward the stable. The stable, deep red and sleek, was the newest addition to our property. The previous summer, Dad's crew descended on the place and built the large and modern-looking building to house Dad's three new investments. Before Dad had the money to buy this land and build this house and the stable, we lived in Grandpa and Grandma's old house. Dad and Mom and my sisters moved in after Grandma's health got worse and to take care of her and Grandpa, though once Grandpa yelled at Dad to remember that he and Mom moved in because they were broke and I was on the way.

"Did they even look you in the eye in the courtroom?" I asked as I broke into a jog to keep up with Dad's long, determined strides. I wanted to hear about all the drama of the trial. I didn't know anybody with a parent who was getting sued. It seemed scandalous and exciting.

"These men, these Jorges and Juans and Joses, they sneak into our country and take jobs away from hardworking Americans," he said, and his words trumped mine. "Then they complain that we're not being fair to them. You can't come into my country, take from my people, and talk to me about fair."

"Were you mad when you saw them in the courtroom?"

"Sure, of course. I wish I never hired the ungrateful bastards. I gave them a start here. They took that for granted," he said without looking up as he dumped hay into Pony Up's stall.

"I guess if you never gave them the jobs, you could have given them to Americans," I pondered and rested my arms on the wooden gate until Dad pushed through it to move on to the next horse.

"I couldn't give them the jobs if they didn't come here in the first place," Dad said, and his logic seemed good.

But then I thought about it a bit more. "So why did you hire them? You could hire other people, people from here."

Dad stood up, still holding a clump of hay like he was building a nest, and looked at me. When he got a serious look on his long face and his eyes shined a little, he looked like the horses. "Because they're willing to work for dirt. I can't argue with that. That's capitalism, Ruthie. You'll learn that when you get older. Or maybe you won't. But take it from your old man: you've got to learn when to put yourself above the ideals of the country. America's founded on those principles. Looking out for number one is the only way to survive in this world."

I wasn't sure if I followed what Dad was saying anymore. We were supposed to be patriots but we were supposed to protect our wealth too, even if that meant going against our patriotism. I wanted to ask him to explain it again, but he looked tired. He probably spent all day talking in court. I didn't want to upset him.

"They're green lawyers—can you believe that?" Dad asked, and it seemed maybe he wasn't done talking. The horses and I were his only audience, and we were all listening. "They say they're fighting the good fight as environmental lawyers, but they do it for the money like everyone else. They care about the green of their dollar bills more than the green of the rainforest or wherever it is they're 'saving.' The lead lawyer's name is Oakleaf. An environmental lawyer named Oakleaf. Here I thought I had heard it all," he said and laughed like a man with no worries in the world.

"How come environmental lawyers are suing your drywall company?" I asked. "Did you do something bad to the land?"

Maybe since my grandpa was no longer around for Dad to talk to about it, he was finally ready to talk to me: "They handle other cases too. Employment law. They made their reputation taking on big corporations. Don't know why they lump my company in with Wal-Mart. There's no more than a hundred of us. These bastards try and tell me I'm some evil businessman, but I started the same place as my employees, laying drywall and building this company from the ground up, all by myself."

Dad finished feeding the horses and looked at them while he wiped his gloved hands together. I stood beside him and waited for him to speak again, but instead he turned and walked out the door without looking at me.

Dad thought the case was a sure deal. He told his lawyers he wouldn't settle. *Let the fence-hoppers come to court.* Dad said he wanted to see an honest, red-blooded American sitting on that jury convict him of a crime for making a bunch of lazy Mexicans work harder.

Grandpa once told me, "The way I see it, your father thinks there is only one right way to look at things—his." Grandpa never said "my son," always "your father." Maybe this was accidental, but I figured Grandpa knew too much about how words worked to have used them carelessly.

Dad bought our three horses from a broker he met at Emerald Downs, where he and my brothers-in-law liked to go on Sundays: Pony Up, Lightning Speed, and Yellow Sam, whose name later got changed to Dandelion when my niece Whitney fell off her bike in our driveway and the only way Dad could calm her down enough to bandage her knees was to let her to rename the female horse. My sisters never brought up Cletus, but I thought about it. I guess Dad softened a bit.

The horses hadn't performed well for months, but he figured he could bring them back to our custom-built stable and rest them up. The night the trucks brought them, I stood on the porch and watched him guide the horses, holding them gently by the reins and walking them into their new home.

"The trick is to put the horse back out there in a year or so and let him perform badly. It's good for him to lose at first. In the smaller races, the faster horses get handicapped with weights to slow them down, which means my horses will eventually get their stride back and win. So all I have to do is bet on them with their low odds and make sure nobody else sees them as good competitors. The payout will be huge. Of course, there's always breeding as an option. It's good to have a backup plan."

During the trial, Dad spent most nights by himself in the stable. Grandpa died not long after the subpoena was served, so Dad spent his time ranting to the horses. I spent most nights answering calls from my sisters and their husbands; Aunt Raylene and Uncle Jeff; and the occasional distant relative calling for gossip.

"Oh Ruthie, I hate to say it because he's my brother, but he probably deserves to pay for this. I've heard the charges: no rest breaks, unpaid overtime. He's been working those poor sons of bitches to the bones for years 'cause he thought nobody would complain. Probably thought it was a good system—why would a bunch of undocumented immigrants want any attention from the courts? I guess they got pushed too far. Sometimes a man gets away with something so long he gets to thinking he's invincible," Aunt Raylene said to me during one of her calls, her voice velvety with the bottle of red wine everyone in the family knew she drank nightly.

Dad cried the night he came home with the verdict. I had only seen him cry three times—when our dog Lucy got hit by a truck, when Mom left, and when Grandpa died. Mom was around when Lucy got killed, Grandpa was around when Mom left, and I was around when Grandpa died. I hated that I had to be around for Dad again so soon. I wished my aunt or sisters would help. They practically turned their backs on Dad when he got caught up with this case. Couldn't sit through a family dinner without him talking about it, sometimes nothing more than murmuring "my goddamn country" between sips of the six-pack of Rolling Rock he brought for himself during family visits because he didn't like Aunt Raylene and Uncle Jeff's "cheap shit."

Grandpa told me once while Dad was off drying out and he and I were living alone in the house for a month, "If you remember one thing I teach you, Kid, it's that you should blame nobody nor praise them. A man has to live life his own way, just as you will live your life your own way. Don't judge nobody else. Stand on your own two feet and you have a shot of doing right in this world."

I thought it was funny how two people who hated each other could be so similar.

After he died, Dad told me Grandpa used to hit him and Aunt Raylene with a switch growing up. The worst part was that Dad had to pick it from the tree in the backyard first. Sometimes you turn into the person you hate no matter how hard you try not to.

Every winter when I was little, Dad and Mom took my sisters and me to Montana to visit Mom's family. After Mom left and Dad made his money with Care-All Drywall, the trips changed to Mexico, where Dad bought a timeshare in Puerto Vallarta— an expansive hacienda with a tile roof and tile floors, and white curtains in constant motion from the sea breeze. My sisters and I missed Montana—the hot springs, rivers that stretched toward us like extended hands, and Mom's wild family of coal miners. Last we heard, she was living in Montana, so Dad never wanted to go back there again. In Mexico, we cooked fish for dinner, swam at the private beach behind the house, and fought over the one hammock dangling on the back deck. We rarely drove into town or explored the area. Dad talked to the cab drivers and housekeeper when necessary. Dad said he wanted the privacy. *Can't a man get privacy on his own damn vacation?*

On the flights home from Mexico, Dad spent the parts he wasn't sleeping drinking Jack and Cokes and flipping through the *Sky Mall* magazine with the fevered intensity of a child ripping open birthday presents. For years, after every winter trip, our yard bloomed with fountains of little marble boys peeing and lawn gnomes sprouting up like manmade weeds. Even after my sisters left—Rachel first and then Rebecca—Dad and I continued the yearly vacation. The year of the lawsuit, Dad's lawyers advised him not to go. It would appear "insensitive."

One Sunday afternoon, my grandpa called to me from the living room. He was sitting in his recliner with the respirator close by, an accessory of his that had been around so many years it was as unassuming as a cane. I sat down on the new leather couch, my thighs sticking to it in the swampy summer air.

"Kid, I want to tell you a story."

When Grandpa said this, it meant I should get comfortable. I scooted back and leaned into the couch. It felt like the cushion was opening to me, the way butter curls when you slice into it with a knife. I felt the warm heat of the leather, imagined how it once felt when it was the hide of a cow grazing sluggishly on a nearby farm in this same August heat. Grandpa's chair had been around longer than me. It was faded blue corduroy with rips along the seams. "A pathetic thing," Dad called it. Grandpa didn't care.

"I once spent a summer fishing in Alaska. While I was there, I spent some time with the locals. There were a lot of them Indian tribes up there. Some folks integrated with the whites, drinking and shooting the shit at the same taverns as us. Others kept to themselves, real closed off to the rest of society." He pronounced the last word so hard the last syllable drew out to a "tee" that rang through the room like a fork hitting a glass. "One night, one of the guys from a local tribe told me about this elderly woman who had passed. She was the last person who could speak this tribe's language. Can you believe that? An entire language went extinct when she croaked. You think about it with Egyptians or Mayans, those old civilizations. You don't think twice about those languages that are long gone, but to meet the guy who knew someone who was the bearer of an entire language—now that's something. I wish I could have written her obituary. It would have been an honor." He stopped talking when a coughing fit took over, and he looked too tired to say anything more.

That was the last story Grandpa told me before he died from his long battle with lung cancer. Dad let Uncle Jeff place the obituary in the paper. It was two sentences long. Dad threw out the chair a month after the funeral. I hated him for doing that. I locked myself in my room and cried for a night, and he got drunk and passed out in the stable. We were alone together: a father indifferent to his daughter and a daughter whose fear had started boiling toward anger.

I clipped Grandpa's obituary out of the newspaper and added it to the shoebox where I kept other trinkets that reminded me of him: a photograph of him in his uniform, browned and wrinkled from age and family members passing it around like a relic at his funeral; the Purple Heart he left to me; and the obituary he lovingly wrote for my grandma, his own wife:

> The day I met Ruth-Anne, I felt my old self slip away like an animal shedding its winter fur in spring, no longer needed. My heart seized up with excitement the first time she agreed to dance with me. How simultaneously gentle and electrifying a hand can feel when placed in your own. It felt as though my whole life had opened before me like a book you've wanted to read for a long time.
>
> Ruth-Anne was born in the spring. She once told me a woman never reveals her real age, so I'll respect that even in death. She grew up in Lake Stevens and attended college at the University of Washington. She worked as a kindergarten teacher, first in Everett and later in Enumclaw, after settling down with a lucky fool she met at a dance hall. She was an avid reader and painted watercolors and crocheted blankets in her spare time. She loved the fall best and ate every apple her students gave her.
>
> She is preceded in death by a daughter, Emily, who died at birth. She is survived by her hapless husband; her son

Robert and his wife Miranda and their three daughters Rachel, 10, Rebecca, 8, and little Ruth-Anne, 2; and her daughter Raylene Jackson and her husband Jeff Jackson of Federal Way and their sons Mickey, 7, and Brian, 4. She died peacefully at home, surrounded by those she loved. I was lucky to be included amongst that group.

The obituary never made it into the paper; Grandpa had long since retired. But he wrote it out in his cramped, smudgy cursive and kept it tucked away in his desk. I didn't find it until after he died. Sometimes when I stared at Grandma and Grandpa's obituaries, I wondered what Dad's would look like. I bet if Grandpa, Mom, and my sisters and I each wrote our own, they'd all be different. If the men who worked for him wrote one, theirs would be especially damning. But who would get it right? When a person dies, everybody has a different story to tell. Being able to sum up a person's life after death is about as difficult as it is to understand them when they're living. Nobody really knows a whole person. After they die, we only tell the parts of them we want to remember: a dad who wanted the best for his girls and raised them the best he could alone, a hard worker. In my version, he didn't need me—he *wanted* me around. Maybe a dead person is just the sum of their best parts.

I stand at the kitchen sink, though the dishes are nearly dry on the rack by now. My fists are in my pockets as I stare out into the black night, searching for movement or a flash of eyes in the yard, a clue of what's to come. The front door slams shut, and I shudder.

"Get your boots," Dad yells from the hallway.

I peek my head out of the kitchen but don't say a word. Dad has that look on his face like he's not looking to answer any questions.

"Hurry up, Ruth-Anne," he shouts, and I run to the front door for my boots. He disappears down the hall to his bedroom and comes back with the shotgun. I can smell the sweet gasoline odor of booze on him as he passes me and walks straight out the front door.

I run after him, but I don't speak until we enter the stable. The red building appears black at night. The horses look like they were sleeping when Dad flips the switch and a row of bright lights fills the room with an artificial glow. It smells like wood chips and horseshit inside.

Even though I know the answer, I ask anyway: "What are you going to do?"

"I'm going to shoot them, all of them. A dead horse is good to nobody. They think they can come on my land and take my home, my property, and now my goddamn horses. I'll burn the house down if I have to. I'll watch it all burn before I let a bunch of strangers take what's mine. We'll start with the horses."

"But Dad, you can't. The horses didn't do anything," I say, but I know innocence never had anything to do with this.

"Tell that to the lawyers. They did this. A man can't be pushed like this without pushing back."

He shoots Dandelion first, which seems like a special kind of cruel. Or maybe he did it because she was Whitney's and he wanted to surprise her so she wouldn't feel scared right before she died. Pony Up and Lightning Speed whinny and begin thrashing inside their stalls. They run in small circles, kicking up dirt that clouds the air. I think maybe Dad will stop now that he's seen how scared the others are, but he doesn't stop. Dad takes a step toward Lightning Speed and points the gun at his head. His hands are shaking, but he steadies himself and breathes deeply. The first shot for Dandelion sobered him up a bit. He moves the gun in a straight line from the muzzle up to the forehead. It only takes one shot when you're that close.

I turn and bend down to vomit. It's happening too fast. My ears are ringing from the gunshots and the horses' screams. I begin to cry. Then I feel Dad's hand on my shoulder.

"Stand up," he says.

My knees tremble beneath me, so I hold onto him as I rise. I look to him for confirmation that it's over. He takes his hand away from me and reaches into his pocket to pull out two more shotgun shells, though there's only one horse left. He reloads the gun, and turns it around so that I can grab for the stock. I cover my mouth with the back of my hand. The smell of blood creeps into my nostrils and I begin to heave again.

"Come on, take it. The sooner you do this, the sooner it will be over," he says and stabs the air with it like he's poking a bear.

I reach unsteadily for the gun. He thrusts it into my hand. "Why do I have to shoot him?"

"Prove to me you have what it takes. You're the only one who's left, the only one who stood by me in this. Not my goddamn wife, my sister, my own father," he says.

Pony Up isn't running around as much, but he whinnies and whips his head. Both his big, jewel-like eyes focus on me. I could take the gun and run. Or I could tell him no for once and call the police. I could fling open the stall door and let him run. Or I could shoot him and end this.

"You can do this," he says and covers his mouth, swaying a bit, from the drinking or what's happened, I'm not sure. *Make your dad proud.* He staggers a few steps toward Pony Up's stall as if to show me that he's right here, he's right here waiting for it.

My eyes blur from crying. How can anyone expect me to see if I'm crying? I'm hysterical, "got the hysterics" as Dad says.

A man needs a legacy, someone to carry on his name. You have a bunch of girls and what do they do but abandon their own father. I should've had boys.

So then I think, I can still shoot even with the hysterics. I can see where the horse stands; I can see where Dad stands. I just have to stop my hand from shaking, which is hard to do with him yelling at me like that.

"Gimme the damn thing. Want anything done in this world, you do it yourself." He walks toward me.

Look out for number one. I can survive in this world.

He starts to grab it from me, and between that and the crying, and the horse's screaming like he's got the hysterics too, what can I do but pull the trigger? When I watch him fall to the ground to huff and kick around in the dirt, he stirs up so much dust my eyes sting all over again, and I think maybe it's best for him. Sometimes you've got to put down an old creature, put him out of his misery.

SO BE IT

The Mac Attack Stack Challenge is the pride of Lloyd's BBQ City and Auction House in Zillah, Washington. You start with a double-double-decker hamburger—that's four quarter-pound Angus beef patties, cooked medium-rare. You nestle these puppies on a hamburger bun like they're angels resting on a cloud in heaven—a cloud soaked in a half stick of butter. Then you've got your usual burger culprits: pickles, onion, tomato, and lettuce, plus a generous slab of special sauce, which everybody knows is just ketchup and mayonnaise. The cherry on top is two thick-cut slices of bacon.

Just when you think Lloyd's BBQ is giving you nothing more than your run-of-the-mill heart-attack burger, the wizards in the kitchen add a scoop (an *ice cream* scoop) of Lloyd's famous homemade mac and cheese. This is no ordinary mac and cheese like your grandma makes. It's elbow pasta topped with mild cheddar, sharp cheddar, a good helping of Velveeta, plus a sprinkling of bread crumbs for crunch. The molten mac and cheese oozes down the burger, turning it into a mouthwatering masterpiece. Add a pound of fries on the side, and you've got the Mac Attack Stack Challenge. Here's the kicker: you've only got thirty minutes to wolf down this beauty. Do this, and you get your picture on Lloyd's Wall of Fame. Since the challenge started back in 2002, roughly one hundred people have tried, and less than half have finished.

Bonnie felt the heat immediately. The six-hour bus ride from Portland to Yakima, where her dad waited to pick her up and drive her back down to Toppenish, had shielded her from the June swelter. But as soon as she stepped down from the bus, and for those five minutes of waiting, walking, and loading her stuff into her dad's truck, she felt sweat form a thick layer on her skin.

"Your first day back home, college girl. Got any big plans?" her dad asked her when the country music station went to commercials.

"Nothing yet. I might give it a day before I start texting people." She watched Yakima roll by as they sped along the freeway, past the quickly growing cornfield that would be cut into the haunted corn maze in the fall to provide thrills for kids and dark hiding places for horny teens, then through the break in the hills that caused static to briefly overtake the radio, and on to the Lower Valley.

"That's what I hoped you would say. I've got a little surprise in store for you, but I was willing to wait if you already made other plans." He smiled and rested his left arm on the open window.

She rolled her window down too and let her hand wave across the wind as she listened to the returning music. She didn't enjoy her dad's musical selections, but she preferred listening to talking.

"Aren't you going to ask me what the surprise is?"

"No. You won't tell me if I do."

"Smart girl," he said and turned the music up a little louder.

The house that Bonnie and her father returned to that afternoon was the same house she had returned to her whole life, starting with the day her parents first brought her home from the hospital. The marked difference now was the absence of her mother. In the two years since her mother's passing, her absence had taken a noticeable toll on the house. Her mother had kept the bookshelves free of dust, the refrigerator stocked with wholesome foods, and the carpet vacuumed.

When Bonnie's dad opened the front door and she walked inside for the first time since winter break, Bonnie breathed in the stale air and coughed.

"Sorry. I forgot to turn the AC on," her dad explained and rushed past her and into the hallway to fiddle with the air conditioning.

She dropped her bag in the hallway even though her bedroom was only a few feet down the hall. Moving to the kitchen, she reached for the sink faucet and stuck her head under a cool stream of water. When she brought her head back up, Bonnie scanned the area: food-crusted dishes piled on the counter near the dishwasher, scuffs on the carpet from wearing shoes indoors, and mail and catalogues stacked in sagging piles.

She reached for the refrigerator door and pulled it open to find it stocked with packaged bacon, ground beef, and hot dogs. The sight of so much meat made her stomach drop. Bonnie had become a vegetarian only weeks after starting freshman year at Reed College in Portland. Becoming a vegetarian was almost as much a rite of passage as losing your virginity or smoking your first joint, all of which she had done within the first month of the first semester.

"Whoa, not so fast," her dad said and put his hand over hers, pushing the refrigerator door shut. "We're going out for dinner tonight."

She dropped her hand and thought of the nearby restaurants in Toppenish: the buffet at the local casino, the family diners, and the fast-food chains. "I'm not sure I'm up for eating in Toppenish tonight."

"Not Toppenish. We're driving over to Zillah to go to Lloyd's," he replied with a puffed-up chest.

"Is that the place where they sell furniture in the same building as the restaurant?"

"Auction it; it's not a furniture store. If that were the case, they'd be my direct competition, and I, my princess, would be a traitorous king to eat there." He stood in front of the refrigerator like he was guarding it.

Bonnie's dad owned a furniture store in Toppenish. Her whole life, he had been "King Ben," owner and spokesperson for the Furniture Emporium and Mattress Warehouse. For as long as she could remember, his commercials appeared on the local TV stations. He wore a velvet costume he had invested in years before and made "royal proclamations" about the newest leather sectionals in stock, or the big Memorial Day sale. In one commercial, a five-year-old Bonnie had acted out *The Princess and the Pea* on top of a pile of mattresses. Her dad still had it on VHS.

"Okay, so why are we going there? Is there an auction tonight?" She left the kitchen and wandered into the living room.

"Nope, no auction. We're going for the food and the food alone," he answered, following behind her and piling the mail into taller stacks like he was playing Jenga.

"Any special reason?" She picked up a framed family portrait from when she was ten and still allowed her parents to drag her into portrait studios. She ran a thumb across her mother's face, swiping away a thin film of dust.

"Because, Bonnie my dear, tonight your old man has a date with destiny."

There was the hot wings challenge in the Tri-Cities—attempted and won on the second try. It's not the amount of food that causes the trouble, but the level of spiciness in the wing sauce. The cook at the wings joint calls it "Devil's Sauce," and the moment it hits your lips, you feel the hellfire burn. The trick is to pull all the meat off the bones first with a fork so you can scoop it in without letting it touch your skin. Unfortunately, you learn that trick the hard way, which is why you need the second attempt. There was the chilidog challenge in Yakima, which was an easy victory, but full of later consequences. Let's just say that the T-shirt you won wasn't quite worth the pain. Ellensburg's rib challenge falls on the same weekend as the rodeo, so you're up against cowboys, rodeo clowns, and Old West wannabes. What a motley crew to dig into all those ribs, sucking BBQ sauce off the tips of their fingers or wiping it off their faces with the back of their hands—there is no time for delicacy in a rib contest. There is only one winner standing and bowing before a pile of bones, and a bunch of other chumps reaching for wet wipes.

To compete in the oyster-eating contest put on by a seafood restaurant on the Puget Sound, you have to drive almost three hours to Seattle. It's worth it, though, to watch the bulging eyes on the other contestants as they stuff themselves to the gills with those slimy little creatures. That annual event, held in the height of summer travel season, brings in fishermen and tourists alike. The fishermen, gritty and hungry, open their mouths and let the oysters slide down their throats like mother's milk. The tourists, usually insurance salesmen from South Dakota, sunburnt on their noses because they didn't plan for sun in the Pacific Northwest, give their cameras to their wives and ask them to take pictures. When an out-of-towner, raised on meat and potatoes, overestimates his stomach and tries to slurp down too many oysters, you can only hope his wife snaps a shot of him puking his guts into the complimentary sick bucket.

Bonnie's parents were both raised as Jehovah's Witnesses. Throughout her life, they tried to explain to her all of the good things that came from being a Jehovah's Witness, about the paradise on earth that someday awaited her. Throughout all of this placating, Bonnie only ever thought of the things she could not have or do. There were no holidays—no Christmas trees, no homemade Halloween costumes—and no birthdays to celebrate. Bonnie wasn't even allowed to attend her friends' birthday parties until she turned thirteen and threw such an epic tantrum— with tears and slamming doors and the promise of ending her life unless she was allowed to attend her best friend's birthday sleepover—that her parents caved on the issue.

But the Jehovah's Witnesses had no food restrictions. Restrictions on your sexuality and drugs, yes. Even one against saying the Pledge of Allegiance and playing school sports. But nothing like Mormons and caffeine, Catholics and meat on Fridays, or Muslims and pork. When Bonnie's mom had to excuse her from the school's Christmas pageant, she took her to Dairy Queen for Dilly Bars during the performance. After Bonnie complained that her parents were still allowed to celebrate their anniversary, they came up with an alternative celebration to birthdays and holidays called "Bonnie's Day" that they held in July and celebrated with a sheet cake from Costco with buttercream frosting. When she had to stay home from the homecoming dance, Bonnie's dad let her have as much Dr. Pepper and Cool Ranch Doritos as she wanted while she stayed up to sneak *Saturday Night Live.*

One of the other central restrictions in the Jehovah's Witness religion was the transfusion of blood. Because the blood is sacred, it should not be shared between two bodies. When Bonnie's parents were driving home from dinner on Highway 97 the night the driver of a semi-truck hauling milk, who should have stopped overnight in Yakima, dozed off and veered his truck across the road and into Bonnie's dad's truck, Bonnie's mom refused to have the blood transfusion that would have saved her life. Bonnie was seventeen years old and just starting to enjoy the ninety-degree heat of the start of her summer vacation when her mom died in the emergency room in the Sunnyside hospital.

Bonnie began applying early to colleges weeks after her mom's funeral. Neither of her parents had attended college, nor did their siblings or their parents. When you follow a religion that says the world is going to end any minute now, you don't look that far into the future. Some of her cousins had dropped out of high school; one had gotten married at fifteen and left school to start having babies. With all the restrictions, all the things they said she couldn't do, after her mom died, Bonnie immediately felt the need to go to college. It was part rebellion, part desire to be different from her family, and part consuming need to leave the town where she had seen her mother—stubborn and devout (and Bonnie had never been angrier with her for it)—buried in the ground.

Bonnie and her dad rode silently in his truck to the restaurant fifteen minutes away. She feigned nervous excitement over the surprise as a reason for not talking, but really she couldn't think of anything to say to him.

"Here we are, kiddo." Ben parked the truck in the dusty parking lot.

Bonnie pushed open the truck door and hopped onto the gravel. She shielded her eyes from the overpowering evening sun and looked at the big brick building that housed a family restaurant and a giant space full of people's used goods that a fast-talking auctioneer sold to the highest bidder every Wednesday and Sunday night. "LLOYD'S BBQ CITY AND AUCTION HOUSE" was painted in white across the rusty-colored building, announcing in a no-nonsense, straightforward Central Washington way exactly what patrons would find when they entered.

The cool air that hit Bonnie's skin inside was an inviting feeling, as was the iced tea she ordered after she and her dad were seated in a booth near the auction space. She drank the iced tea in gulps as her father more reservedly sipped his Coke.

"So what'll it be tonight, miss?" The waiter, twenty-something and pockmarked, asked while only half-looking at Bonnie.

She ordered a house salad, hold the bacon bits, and looked him dead on. He looked like someone who could have gone to high school with her. Really, he looked like someone anyone went to high school with.

Before he ordered, Bonnie's dad sat up straight in his chair. He gripped his menu with both hands and tapped it against the table like he was straightening a stack of important documents.

Then, while looking straight at his soon-to-be college sophomore and only child, he said, "I'd like to take on the Mac Attack Stack Challenge tonight, son."

Bonnie didn't know what that meant, hadn't seen the sign above the bar that said, "Survive the Mac Attack Stack Challenge, Become a Legend." Bonnie's dad looked at her for recognition of his feat, but she only gave him indifference.

"Aren't you going to ask me about the challenge?" he asked as the waiter disappeared toward the kitchen.

"What challenge? I thought that was the name of your dinner." She refocused her attention to the inside of her bag, where she checked her phone.

"Well, yes, but it's not an ordinary dinner item." He pushed a menu toward her. "Here, read it."

She listed the ingredients out loud, shut the menu, laid it on the table, and rested her hands on top of it. "So what, you're participating in some kind of eating contest?"

"Guilty." He smiled.

"Why?" She had thought that tonight would be as good as any to tell him she had been taking biology classes and was planning to declare it as her major next year. She was even harboring a desire to apply to med school after graduation.

He shuffled in his seat. "Because, kiddo, your old man's got a new hobby."

"So you've done this before? Eating contests?"

"A couple of times," he said, nodding and pursing his lips.

"Have you won?"

He nodded a slow yes.

She accepted that this would not be the night for a serious conversation about her future. They were so good at avoiding those anyway. It was silly of her to expect tonight would be different.

He waved his hand across the table. "I started after you left for college. I went out to dinner in Yakima, and the restaurant there had a food challenge. I tried it on a whim. It was fun, so I tried a few more. I figured tonight, instead of telling you about it, I could show you."

As if on cue, the waiter walked up carrying a tray of food, followed by a large man with a bald head, and handed the dinners to Bonnie and her dad. Bonnie looked from her plate to the waiter and then to her father, whose seemingly detached head floated above a burger four patties high and covered in a waterfall of cheese.

"Ladies and gentlemen, fine patrons of Lloyd's BBQ City and Auction House, tonight, we have a challenger," the bald man said with a thin glaze of sweat sheening his skin. He grabbed Bonnie's dad by the upper arm and yanked him from the table. "Stand up, stand up," he said amidst a small burst of applause from the half-filled tables. "What's your name?"

"My name is Ben Adams." Ben looked around the room and nodded at strangers.

The man pushed Ben back down and said, "Well, Ben, let me give you the rules of the Mac Attack Stack Challenge. You have thirty minutes to finish the burger, mac and cheese, and side of fries. No getting up, no going to the bathroom—if you puke, it doesn't count. If you win, you get fame and adoration. If you lose, you owe me thirty bucks for the whole meal. That's it." He looked between Bonnie and her dad and then said amusedly, "And no sharing."

There were a few more cheers before the man set a timer on the table and told them he'd check in at the five-minute mark. The waiter and the bald man walked away from the table and left them with their food.

"Who was that?" Bonnie asked.

"That's Big Dog, the owner. He's the only one who cooks

up the challenge, and there are certain nights when he's in the kitchen, like tonight," Ben explained hurriedly as he pulled his plate closer.

Bonnie began picking at her wilted lettuce and two cherry tomatoes. "Where's Lloyd?"

"He's long gone. Big Dog's his son. He's the madman who came up with this challenge. Created it in honor of his father. So I have to blame him if this puppy gets the best of me." He pointed at the burger with both hands, drawing Bonnie's eyes to the plate, as if to say, "Look at this. Look what I'm doing."

"Shouldn't you get started? At least three minutes have gone by."

"Good point. See, this is why I need you here. You look out for your old man." Ben's eyes scrutinized the plate. He picked up his knife and fork, one in each hand.

"Ladies and gentlemen, esteemed customers of Lloyd's BBQ City and Auction House, tonight is a very special night," Big Dog boomed a few tables away over a plate identical to Ben's and a man who sat behind it, nodding at his friends. Big Dog pulled him out of his seat. He looked about twenty-two and was ginger-haired, sunburnt on his cheeks and nose, and wearing an American Eagle T-shirt. He looked like he went to the state college in Pullman.

After the frat boy said his name—Paul—Big Dog rattled off the same instructions, slapped Paul on the back, and shoved him back into his seat. Then Big Dog turned back to Ben, whose fork and knife hovered above an untouched burger at the twenty-six minute mark, and said, "Looks like you've got more than a burger for a competitor tonight." The frat guy's table erupted into cheers and the smashing together of beer bottles.

You've got to have technique. Without technique, you're walking into a challenge unprepared. Very few can just wing it and win. Maybe luck and a big stomach gets you through some of the easier challenges, but you don't win a biggie like the Mac Attack Stack Challenge without a plan. You've got to know how to make the most of your time, since your stomach will hit a wall at the twenty-minute mark. Forget thirty minutes; twenty is the magic number.

It's almost like an art. Maybe it's all just spatial planning, something that comes in handy at the furniture store: the sofas go across from the entertainment centers; bigger sofa equals bigger entertainment center. Potential customers don't want to see a living room that looks off-balance. If they don't see it right in the store, they can't imagine it in their own home. So with this challenge, you have to think how best to face it. First you start by breaking down the parts. Divide and conquer. Think of it this way: there are three main components that can be tackled individually. Start by scraping the mac and cheese off the burger to let it cool down and avoid burning your tongue. Then break the burger down into two open-faced sandwiches, two patties each. It looks unmanly, sure, but it goes by faster if you use your fork and cut the burger into smaller bites. Then if you're slugging along for a while, you can dip the bite of burger into the mac and cheese or stack a fry or two on top to wake up your taste buds.

And don't forget to chase every couple of bites with a swig of something. It makes it easier to swallow all that food.

Some childish desires don't go away, like the inexplicable joy of kicking a pinecone along the sidewalk. Bonnie's dad ate his first half of the giant hamburger with wide eyes. He pierced four, five, six French fries at a time. He ate gleefully, without pausing to wipe his face with a napkin. He ate like someone who thought nobody was watching. Bonnie sipped her iced tea until she reached the bottom and kept sipping, sucking air from the bottom of the glass. She kept sipping until her dad looked up at her like she was embarrassing him.

"Are you doing okay?" Bonnie asked him. That was a question meant to show she was engaged in the challenge, in this father-daughter moment he had set up for them to share. But the way she said it, or else the way he looked at her like he thought she said it, made it seem like it was a broader question than how he was doing in that moment.

"This is a tough one."

When Bonnie stood in the hospital room with her father, overlooking her mom's color-drained face, she waited for some kind of explanation, some apology for refusing to live. Bonnie's mom looked past her husband and daughter and said, "So be it." Her last words whispered and the last heard by her resentful daughter. It was such utter acceptance that, at the time, Bonnie called it defeat. Her mother gave up. She just gave up.

A silence existed between Bonnie and Ben for months after. Dinner was drowned out by the sound of the television. Car rides were filled with radio static. In the mornings during Bonnie's senior year, Ben would cook breakfast—eggs, pancakes, and bacon—and make up a plate for Bonnie, but she grabbed a granola bar and ran to her bus.

The silence was made easier, less obvious, once Bonnie moved away for college. The silence became accidentally forgetting to return a phone call. Moving on with her new friends and classes was as easy as hitting "ignore" on her cell phone. She skipped returning home for spring break in favor of spending the week at the Oregon Coast with her best friend. She didn't ask her dad how things were going at the store or what he had been up to lately. His absence was more active than her mother's, richer and full of more anger. It was hard to hate someone who's dead; the living took the blow.

Bonnie finished her salad and rested the fork on her napkin. She watched her dad stop eating and stare at his plate. Half of the burger and all of the fries were gone. He had split the second half of the burger into two pieces and held one loosely between his thumb and forefinger. She tried not to see the sweat pooling on his forehead and above his upper lip. Instead, she scanned the room, past the tables filled with families chewing steaks and baked potatoes with the lazy movements of cows and onto the deer heads mounted above the restrooms—"Bucks" and "Does."

Like a traitor, she let her eyes wander to the competitor's table. His plate was clear of everything but the fries.

"He had a better plan. He saved the fries for last," her dad said when he caught her looking.

She turned back to him. "Why does that matter?"

"It just does, believe me. I was too chaotic, started picking at everything at once. The fries are carbs, filler. I should have finished the meat first and ended with the fries. But he threw me off. I didn't think someone else would compete." His voice whimpered, sounding apologetic.

She straightened in her chair and looked him dead-on. "So what? He doesn't matter. You're not competing against him. You're competing against yourself."

You've got to hunker down and plow through. Five minutes to the threshold. You've got to beat the food. You don't think it's important at first. You think, this is just fun, no big deal if I don't do it. But the first time you lose, you realize it is about something more. It's bigger than you thought. The winning is more important than you ever thought. It's something. You've got to have something.

You look at your life. You've got a wife—gone. You've got a daughter, here but not really. Sure, you've got a good job, but what's a job after five? Sometimes you wonder why God didn't take you instead, or as well. You can't be selfish, for the kid's sake, but sometimes you feel selfish. You let your selfish thoughts ease you into sleep at night. Sometimes it feels like they're all you've got. Then, in the stillness that comes late at night, you wonder if there was ever a God to begin with. And if there wasn't, how could you let the love of your life go?

The food becomes this thing, this need you've got to fill. You look at your daughter sitting across the table from you, and dammit if she's not perfect. How did we make this perfect creature? She's this perfect, smart, stubborn child who refuses to let you pull one over on her. What do I do with her now? She looks at you like you're some kind of idiot, like she really pities you. So you keep eating. It's something to prove to her. You prove to her that you can do this. And it doesn't make sense. It doesn't make sense, but you keep eating because nothing makes sense anymore.

Bonnie's dad sat with the hamburger bite drooping between his fingers. He breathed out and sunk lower in his chair.

Big Dog came barreling back out of the kitchen at the four-minute mark. "Come on, Ben. You've got less than five minutes to go. Two bites of burger and a couple scoops of macaroni left," he said in a loud voice as he slapped Ben on the back. Then he leaned in and whispered, "That kid over there, he's ahead of you. Are you really going to let some punk kid beat you?"

Ben shook his head.

Big Dog stood back up and faced the restaurant. "Come on, everybody: Ben, Ben, Ben." The room broke into half-sincere chanting. Bonnie watched the waiter refill her glass of iced tea and wondered how many of these displays he had to watch each week.

Ben finished the second-to-last bite of burger by dropping it on a spoonful of macaroni. He paused and took a drink of Coke, swishing it around in his mouth. He kept his eyes on the plate, not on the clock that was counting down from two minutes. Even if he stuffed all the food in his mouth, he wouldn't be able to chew it in time—Bonnie could tell just by looking at him. For as tall a man as her dad was, when he felt embarrassed, he slouched his shoulders and looked like he was desperately trying to force his big body to shrink.

It was then that the cheering erupted at the frat guy's table. It started as a low roar, the testosterone-driven grunts that grew outward, picking up the oohs and ahhs of nearby tables, the indifferent applause from the underappreciated waitstaff. Ben stopped chewing and looked over his shoulder. Only then did Bonnie allow herself to look too.

Only one fight occurred between them after Bonnie's mother's death. It happened when Bonnie received her acceptance letter to Reed. It started out as a conversation about paying for college, twisted into Bonnie's dad reminding her how he felt about her going away to school, and escalated into Bonnie denouncing her religion in one fireworks moment.

"*Your* religion killed my mother," she yelled and pointed her finger at him as they stood in the kitchen. She gripped her acceptance letter in her other hand like a lifeline. That's when it dawned on her that it was, in fact, her parents' religion and never her own. It was something they had passed down to her like a family tradition, an heirloom, like that dark oak armoire that had moved from her grandma's house into her parents' house and would someday end up in her own.

He did not respond.

This was the kind of fight you never came back from. Those things had been said—they couldn't be unsaid, couldn't be taken back, forgotten. When she graduated college and her dad clapped for her in the audience, when he walked her down the aisle at her wedding, when he held his first grandchild in his hands: during any of these times and at every visit and uncelebrated birthday, the words would live below the surface, simmering underneath every pleasantry.

"Paul, Paul, Paul," the crowd chanted. The buzz of Ben's countdown had sounded minutes ago, with the last bite of burger and a few scoops of macaroni left on his plate.

When Ben's face dropped, Big Dog ended his supportive chanting and turned the audience's attention onto Paul—not, it seemed, in disappointment of Ben's loss, but to distract the crowd from it.

At the one-minute mark, Paul ate the last bite. He chewed with an open mouth, smiling as the crushed beige of French fries spread across his teeth.

"Ladies and gentlemen, we have a champion," Big Dog said and rushed to the table. He grabbed Paul's arm like he was a heavyweight champ and pulled him from his seat. Paul jumped up and down with both arms in the air, cheering like he had tackled his first keg stand.

Amid the "woos," Paul stopped jumping and clutched his stomach. He bent over like he had been sucker punched. He looked between his friends' smiling faces and turned to run. His friends jumped out of their seats and followed him to the "Bucks" sign.

"If he throws up, it doesn't count. The rule is you've got to keep it down," Big Dog called to the fleeing frat boys. He swiped at the air with a dismissive wave and walked back to the kitchen.

Ben turned back to the table and met his daughter's eyes. "Well, you can't win 'em all." He stood up and pulled the napkin he had ceremoniously tucked into his shirt collar and dropped it on the table. "Come on, if we hurry back home, maybe you'll still have time to go out with your friends. I'm sure you'd rather see them than hang out with your old man. You can take the truck."

Bonnie rarely saw her dad cry. She never once heard him question his wife's decision to die. He could have a heart attack and die right now, and Bonnie would barely know who this man was. If they hadn't been cosmically forced into a familial relationship, they wouldn't have liked each other. But they were alone, together, and that was the best either of them would get.

Bonnie watched her dad as he pulled out his wallet to pay the ridiculous amount of money he owed for his failure. She picked up her fork and stabbed a piece of macaroni. Ben didn't ask her why, but he did sit back down.

"We might as well finish what we started," she said.

She placed forkfuls of lukewarm cheese and gummy pasta into her mouth as her dad stuffed the last bite of burger into his own, letting a drop of ketchup pool at the corner of his mouth and not bothering to wipe it away.

SIBLINGS AND OTHER DISAPPOINTMENTS

"Remember what Mom used to say about babies?" Elizabeth asks her brother.

He swallows his beer, scratches his stomach. "No, I don't remember. What did she say?"

"Maybe she never told you, because you're a boy, but she used to tell me all the time that babies were these little seeds that God planted in our stomachs."

"That's endearing, I guess."

"No, it was terrifying. Every time I had a stomachache, I thought a garden was growing inside me."

Elizabeth is coming up on two months here at her brother's place in Coeur d'Alene, in the house they grew up in that he took over after Mom died. It's been two and a half months since Scott left her. It's been four months since her daughter died. She counts time now in relation to the accident. Soon it will be six months. Someday it will be a year, and someday even further out, if she's lucky, she'll make it to a whole decade. The therapist Scott wanted her to see told her to think of everything in terms of steps. All the steps counted, even the little ones.

She's getting up in the mornings now. The first month here, she didn't leave her room before noon. But it's summer and the mornings are brighter, and she can't stay in bed with all the light streaming through the windows. Her brother, Ray, is always up before her. For a drunk, he's an early riser. Sometimes she catches him drinking a beer in the morning, and then she wonders if he ever went to bed at all. It bothers her most of the time, but he was the only one to offer her a place to stay after she moved out of her apartment, so she can't complain.

In the kitchen, he's sitting at the table holding yesterday's paper. She whacks him on the back of the head and says, "You smoke too much. It's gonna kill you." She reaches out and grabs his cigarette from the ashtray.

"You could ask for one. You don't have to have just the butt of mine."

"I shouldn't have a whole one. I hate that I'm even smoking again. God, if Scott saw me, he'd be so disappointed. He hated this vice."

"Caroline loved all mine, so much that she made them all her own."

Ray's wife left him five years back. She gave him three tries to sober up, three trips to rehab, and then she left him. She wasn't as bad off as Ray, but it was still a low thing leaving him in the night like that, especially when she used to be the one drinking right beside him.

"Do you want anything to eat?" he asks his sister.

"What did you have?" She's sitting across from him and she puts her legs up on the chair next to her while she smokes. She's getting used to living like this. In her old life she would have showered by now and already been at work. But in this life she doesn't wash her hair as often, and sometimes she forgets about makeup altogether. Her hair has grown a lot lately. She keeps it tied up in a loose bun most of the time during the day, but at night, when she looks at herself in the mirror before bed, she notices that it's past her shoulders. Her hair tracks time with her.

"Eggs, toast," he answers.

"I'm good for now. I just want coffee."

Ever since Ray got laid off last year, he gets an unemployment check in the mail once a month. It's not much, but the house is his and he thinks there's nothing out there for him now. Elizabeth knows she has to go back one day, maybe as soon as the fall, when school starts again, but she tries to think about that as little as possible. For now she likes being around her brother, staying here, and not caring so much about little things like whether she eats breakfast. Scott kept trying to get her to eat, telling her she had to take steps, just little steps.

"Want the paper? I'm on the sports section if you want the news." Ray pushes it toward her.

She pulls it to her but doesn't read it. Her brother doesn't care what she eats or drinks or does or doesn't do. He said she could stay as long as she wants.

Ray and Elizabeth lose track of each other in the middle of the day. He spends most afternoons chopping firewood or sleeping. She's started taking more walks through the woods on the edge of the neighborhood. She likes the feeling of almost getting lost in the pines but trusting she'll eventually find her way out.

She knows this neighborhood well: the sidewalks and the street names, the old man in the blue house next door who used to complain about their basketball hoop, even the hill she and her friends rode their bikes down without helmets.

Her brother is a decade older than her, so they experienced childhood at different times. By the time she was learning to ride a ten-speed and having sleepovers, he was getting kicked out of school for drinking on the baseball field during lunch. He left the house at eighteen and disappeared for most of his twenties. She spent most of her twenties earning her teaching certificate and getting married and only saw him the few times she visited him in rehab.

Now that she spends her time tracking days, Elizabeth wonders if that was how Ray survived his time in rehab. Did he keep a calendar in his room and mark each finished day with an X? Each X moved him toward his release from rehab, toward something—a beginning. If she were to do the same, she would only be marking her movement away from an ending.

"I never took you out for your twenty-first birthday," he thinks out loud as they split a six-pack over dinner.

"No, you never did. I think you sent me a card." She used to keep the letters he sent her from rehab, even those silly beaded necklaces he made her—the product of a sober and suddenly bored life.

"Sorry about that, Beth."

"You know, I don't think we'd ever had a drink together until I moved in. I kind of always resented your drinking, so I never wanted to do it with you."

"I've got it under control now." He's said this before. Elizabeth can think of at least two times he's said this exact thing. Both those times were after his first two trips to rehab. He'd come out and the bags weren't as heavy under his eyes, and he'd talk about all the exercise he'd been getting lately, and even though he chain-smoked, he did look a little healthier, had that glow of the newly detoxified.

"Yeah, I guess it's different now," she says as a sort of half lie. It's not as bad as it used to be, but she doesn't know if it's gotten better or less obvious. Elizabeth made the trip with their mother to drop him off and pick him up from rehab the first two times because Caroline refused to do it. Elizabeth didn't come the third time.

"It was worse with Caroline." Ray looks down and goes back to eating. He's always eaten a lot, but now it's starting to stick to him.

"I know, Ray," she mutters, almost apologetically. She remembers the times with Caroline. She heard most of the stories secondhand from Mom, but occasionally Ray would call her up when it was really bad, like the time Caroline threatened to kill herself or the time he hit her and she called the cops. They never had little fights, the two of them, and then one day their marriage imploded.

Then again, Elizabeth and Scott never really fought at all— before or after it happened—and look where they ended up.

"Sometimes you just love the wrong person," Ray says when he finds her slumped over on the bathroom floor later that night after the beer is gone.

She doesn't know how her brother knew she was crying about Scott, but she takes his hand anyway. Scott shouldn't have left her like that. She was dealing with it, just in her own way.

Now she thinks about finding her mother in the kitchen when she was five after her dad left and never came back. She thinks of her mother crying and smoking, forgetting to open the window above the sink.

Years later, when she was in high school and had the courage to ask about him, driving home from the rehab after they had dropped off Ray, all her mom said was, "Your father used to make me a lot of promises before he left. Men make a lot of promises at night they don't keep in the morning."

She thinks of these things as Ray helps her walk from the bathroom to the bedroom, and then she falls asleep and dreams of nothing at all.

By the middle of summer, they've found their routine. They always eat breakfast and dinner together. Ray cooks more now that he has someone to cook for, and Elizabeth is slowly finding her appetite. Elizabeth spends her time cleaning out the attic and the garage, clearing out all the stuff they never dealt with after Mom passed. Ray doesn't mind. He tells her he doesn't want to go through it with her, but he's okay with it if she wants to start digging through the mess.

She finds a lot of old photo albums, the kinds of things she thinks Ray should leave out on a coffee table, or a bookshelf at the very least. There is one whole photo album dedicated to the trip they took to California with their mother. It was the only big family vacation they ever took. They spent a day at Knott's Berry Farm. That was Elizabeth's favorite part, but Ray liked the beach better. Mom even paid for him to take a surfing lesson while she read magazines and Elizabeth built sand castles. Elizabeth thinks she should keep this photo album since Ray doesn't seem to care.

She comes down from the attic around seven and sits down to spaghetti and a bottle of merlot. They eat mostly in silence and empty the bottle.

"What do you think Mom would say to us right now if she could see us like this?" Elizabeth asks.

"Well, she wouldn't judge us with her words. She'd leave that up to her eyes," he says, and opens his eyes wide and glares. "Or else she'd spout some biblical wisdom for us. Remember how much scripture she could quote?"

"Not just scripture—*Job*. Any problem we had, she gave us Job. I don't know if she did that to make us feel better or worse. Like whatever my problem was, it couldn't be as bad as Job's."

"You know, when Caroline left me, Mom said, 'The Lord has given, and the Lord has taken away.'"

"Jesus Christ, I think she said the same thing to me when our dog Daisy died." She laughs then, and so does he. Their mother probably would have said the same thing after the baby died, but Elizabeth will never know. After the accident was the only time she was happy her mom had passed before her baby was born. How unnatural was it for a grandmother to lose her only grandchild?

Ray grabs two beers from the fridge, and it's like he can tell somehow that her mind has drifted. "Beth," he says quietly, as if he's waking her from a long sleep.

"Yeah?"

He hands her a beer. "Can I ask you about it? The accident, I mean. I've never really asked you about it. I didn't think I was supposed to."

"Sure you can," she says and turns in her chair. She faces him directly.

He looks down at his beer. "Well, what was it like?"

"Honestly, I don't remember much. Scott and I were napping with the baby between us. I remember it being hot that afternoon for March, and the bedroom window had been left open. We were asleep for a long time, and when we woke up, she wasn't breathing. I remember waking up, and I was soaked in sweat. It was just so hot that day."

He leans his chair back, takes a sip of his beer.

"Gosh, can you just imagine what Mom would have said? 'Elizabeth,' she'd say, 'Elizabeth, you actually crushed your own baby. The weight of *you* killed your baby.' That's probably what she'd say." She cups her stomach when she talks.

"She would never say that."

"Yeah, maybe not. But she'd think it. I know she'd think it. I was never good at any of this stuff. Never got that maternal gene."

After a moment he asks, "Do you think you'll go back to work?"

"I don't know. Technically, I'm taking a leave of absence. But I saw the way they all looked at me after it happened. The teachers, the parents. I can't go back there."

"If you didn't go back, where would you go?"

"I haven't figured that out yet. It's so quiet here. I wish I could stay and not go back. I always thought I hated Idaho, but I forgot how quiet it gets out here."

Ray is working through his second beer now. "That's what I always loved too. But Caroline *had* to live in California. She needed the beach and the city and all the noise. She would've never come here with me, even without Mom around. I guess if she hadn't left, I probably never would've made it back here. At least I owe her for that."

Elizabeth drops her beer onto the table. It thuds but doesn't spill. "Look at us. We're so pathetic. We both got left behind. If Mom could see us now, she'd think we're . . ."

"Just like her. We're just like Mom."

"The hell I am. You're more like her than me. You were always more of the nurturer."

"Nurturer?"

"You take care of people, just like Mom. Even if she judged us while doing it, she was still always there when we needed her. She was always *present*. God knows I'm not."

Ray took care of their mom before she died. Sure, he needed a place to crash after the divorce, but he was the one with her up until the very end.

He looks her dead-on. "You're not a bad person, Beth. I hope you hear me saying this. Just because these things have happened doesn't mean you're a bad person. I wish someone would have said that to me."

By her third beer, hours since she last scraped spaghetti sauce off her plate, she's stood up from the table and is wandering through the kitchen, running her hands along the tile counter, picking up and putting down the same pots and pans she remembers her mother cooking with when she was a kid.

"Do you ever think of fixing this place up?" Elizabeth asks him.

"Yeah, all the time. I just don't feel motivated. That's the hard part."

"Could I help you?"

"Are you asking me if you are able to help or if I want your help?"

"Do you want my help?"

"Sure, I guess. I'd love to clear out all that junk behind the house and build a deck. Plus the bathrooms could use new tile. Hell, I wouldn't mind tearing down this wall right here and opening up this space," he says and stands up. He runs his hand along the wall that separates the kitchen and the living room.

She touches the wall too. "We wouldn't have to take the whole wall down. We could put in a pair of French doors. That would really bring the light into the kitchen without turning it into one oversized space." She moves through the room. "Or, if we did take out the wall, we could put in a little island and put up one of those hanging pot racks. Remember how much Mom used to want one of those?"

"Yeah. She always complained that she could never find anything."

"And what about the guest bathroom?"

"Your bathroom?"

"Yes, mine. I think it could use a new showerhead, for one."

He takes a sip of beer and sets it down. Then he moves to the living room. "You know, when Caroline and I were together, we always had these cramped apartments. We never even had a yard of our own. But being here by myself, I never cared enough to fix it up."

"The yard does look awful," she says as she joins him at the back window. It's dark out there now, but she can picture the brown lawn, the drooping plants, and the broken lawn mower.

"Let's look upstairs." He takes the stairs two at a time, and she's running to keep up with him, down the hallway and into his old bedroom, now a storage room. "I've always wanted to turn this into a real study. I want to build bookshelves into this wall here."

She follows him with her eyes and imagines her books lining the wall. "I can see it. And maybe a desk here, and a couple of leather chairs to read in."

"Yeah, yeah, that's just what I was thinking." He stumbles through the doorway and grabs the railing by the stairs. "I want to fix this. I want to fix this place," he says with one big sweep of his arm.

She follows him and looks over the railing at the living room, with the worn floral couch and Mom's old recliner, now Ray's, trying to picture how the house used to look when they were kids.

Elizabeth wants to tell him she's sorry she wasn't there to pick him up the last time he left rehab. She wants to tell him that, but she can't, because it's so late at night and apologies mean more in the morning.

She tells him goodnight and walks to her room. She shuts the door and leans against it in the darkness. She feels tired from the alcohol, but also like she has just woken up. There's a small crashing sound from the kitchen, followed by Ray's cursing.

Lying in bed the next morning, Elizabeth stares at her cell phone with bleary eyes and sends a text to Scott. "I'm sorry. I miss you. I want to come home." She walks downstairs, wrapped in a bathrobe that hasn't been washed in weeks. She sees her brother and stops at the bottom of the stairs. He doesn't see her at first, but she watches him sitting at the table by himself. She sees the empty bottles scattered around the counters—more than there were last night, she thinks. He sits there, staring at the calendar on the wall.

She moves into the kitchen and sits at the table. Ray stands up and starts making the coffee and putting bread in the toaster. She has a worse hangover than he does. Elizabeth rests her head on her hands, but she doesn't feel too terrible—just worn out. Ray settles into his chair with his coffee, but he doesn't pick up the paper yet. He has bags under his eyes; he must have slept less than her. He hasn't mentioned anything about last night. The kitchen is a mess.

After they sit in silence for a few minutes, Ray speaks. "Hey Beth," he says. "I never told you this, but for a while, before I got laid off, I had this job remodeling apartments."

"Yeah?" She's sipping her coffee down fast.

"Basically, me and this other guy would go into apartments that had been trashed and we'd gut and clean them. They were usually apartments that people had been kicked out of or that they cleared out of in the middle of the night without paying for. If somebody shit on their carpet or poured motor oil down their toilet, I had to clean it up."

"God, that's awful. Why are you telling me this?"

"Last night got me thinking about it. Anyway, I was thinking maybe we could go to the hardware store later and start looking at paint samples. I was thinking we could paint your bedroom blue."

She feels a buzz in her bathrobe pocket. She pulls out her phone and reads a text from Scott that says, "miss u too. talk soon?"

"Yeah, we can probably do that, but not now. I'm too tired. Tell me more about this job you had."

He chuckles. "I'll tell you a story about it."

"I don't want to hear about somebody defecating on their carpet, Ray."

"No, it's not that. One time I had to clean out this apartment that this old woman owned. I think she was in her eighties or nineties, just really old. Anyway, she died in the apartment. I don't know how exactly, but nobody found her for two weeks, not until a neighbor complained to the landlord about the smell. The landlord found her. He told me her body looked like Jell-O. I had to go in to work on it, and it still smelled even after we cleaned it. Nothing got it out. It was one of those god-awful smells that lingers in the air, just attaches itself to your clothes and your skin and everything. We had to replace the carpet, even the goddamn walls in that place."

"That's a terrible story," she says.

"I know it is. But it makes a person think."

"Think what?"

"I just don't want to end up alone like that. You know?" Ray stands and fills Elizabeth's cup with the rest of the coffee.

ACKNOWLEDGMENTS

First and foremost, my gratitude to Per and Abbey. You two have been so supportive of me, first as a student of Ooligan, and now as an author. Thank you for believing in this project. To the Ooligan team: what an incredible group of talented, bright, and enthusiastic students. You have made the transition from somebody working inside Ooligan to someone published by Ooligan utterly seamless. Corinne, I am thankful for your savvy, patience, and brilliance. A shout out also to Sophie, Olenka, and Cade and everyone else who invested time and energy into this book.

Thank you to Joaquin, my dear friend, for being an editor, sounding board, and supporter for many of the stories in this collection.

This book, like everything I do, is for my family: Mom, Dad, Alisha, Jacob, Raven, Elias, Adri, and Alex. And for my brother, Justin, this book is a small offering, so little so late. I love you.

Photo by Rachel Kessler

ABOUT THE AUTHOR

Kait Heacock grew up in the same small town as her idol Raymond Carver—she hopes this means something. Kait is a feminist writer and book publicist living in the Pacific Northwest. Her work has appeared in literary journals, magazines, and online, with outlets like *Bustle, DAME Magazine, Esquire, KGB Bar & Lit Mag, Portland Review, tNY.Press, Vol. 1 Brooklyn,* and *The Washington Post.* Kait studied creative writing at Seattle Pacific University and earned her master's degree from Portland State University, where she worked for Ooligan Press. *Siblings and Other Disappointments* is her first book.

OOLIGAN PRESS is a student-run publishing house rooted in the rich literary culture of the Pacific Northwest. Founded in 2001 as part of Portland State University's Department of English, Ooligan is dedicated to the art and craft of publishing. Students pursuing master's degrees in book publishing staff the press in an apprenticeship program under the guidance of a core faculty of publishing professionals. *Italics denote department and project managers.*

PROJECT MANAGER
Sophie Aschwanden
Corinne Gould
Meagan Lobnitz

ACQUISITIONS
Molly K.B. Hunt
Tenaya Mulvihill
Bess Pallares
Sabrina Parys

EDITING
Olenka Burgess
J. Whitney Edmunds
Katey Trnka
Dory Athey
Kristin Choruby
Alex Fus
Emily Goldman
Corinne Gould
Roberta Kelley
Brian Thaden
Theresa Tyree
Alexis Woodcock

DESIGN
Ryan Brewer
Leigh Thomas
Cade Hoover

DIGITAL
Emily Einolander
Cora Wigen

MARKETING
Dory Athey
Jordana Beh
Sophie Aschwanden
Kristin Choruby
Emily Einolander
Alex Fus
Corinne Gould
Cade Hoover
Alexis Woodcock

SOCIAL MEDIA
Alan Scott Holley
Elizabeth Nunes

COLOPHON

Siblings and Other Disappointments is set in Fanwood for the body text, and the headings are set in Halfway. Fanwood is based on the typeface Fairfield, designed in 1940 by Rudolph Ruzicka, a Czech-American type designer, wood engraver, and illustrator. Halfway was created by Indonesian designer Aku Fadhl, and echoes the cover's hand-drawn aesthetic throughout the collection.

CPSIA information can be obtained at www.ICGtesting.com
Printed in the USA
BVOW08s0624070916

461034BV00002BA/6/P